THE MYSTERIOUS DISAPPEARANCE
OF THE MARQUISE OF LORIA

JOSÉ DONOSO

The Mysterious Disappearance
of the Marquise of Loria

*translated from the Spanish
by Megan McDowell*

*with an introduction
by Gabriela Wiener*

A NEW DIRECTIONS
PAPERBOOK ORIGINAL

The translator would like to thank Forrest Gander
for his invaluable contribution in the translation of lines by Rubén Darío.

Originally published in Spanish
as *La misteriosa desaparición de la marquesita de Loria*
by Editorial Seix Barral, S.A., Barcelona, in 1980

First published as New Directions Paperbook 1623 in 2025
Manufactured in the United States of America

Library of Congress Cataloging-in-Publication Data
Names: Donoso, José, 1924–1996, author. | McDowell, Megan, translator.
Title: The mysterious disappearance of the Marquise of Loria / José Donoso ;
translated by Megan McDowell.
Other titles: Misteriosa desaparición de la marquesita de Loria. English
Description: First edition. | New York : New Directions Publishing, 2025. |
Identifiers: LCCN 2024052296 | ISBN 9780811232241 (paperback) |
ISBN 9780811232258 (ebook)
Subjects: LCGFT: Fiction. | Novels.
Classification: LCC PQ8097.D617 M513 2025 | DDC 863/.64—dc23/eng/20241108
LC record available at https://lccn.loc.gov/2024052296

2 4 6 8 10 9 7 5 3 1

New Directions Books are published for James Laughlin
by New Directions Publishing Corporation
80 Eighth Avenue, New York 10011

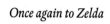

Once again to Zelda

INTRODUCTION

I want to be a Donoso girl

SOMETIMES I HAVE THE UNSETTLING FEELING THAT MY life, and as such my writing, are the product of a queer Chilean man's fevered imagination. And that I have followed the script to a tee and pushed to the limit other people's fantasies, which I believed — and ultimately made — absolutely my own. I'm even more certain that I would have hated having owed a single one of my paraphilias or literary and sexual habits to some *regular* Chilean man. Luckily, that's not the case. The narratives of José Donoso, and later Pedro Lemebel, were my foundational dissident readings — first in the closet, then as part of the queer *marica* carnival — and all those stories burned inside me until they compelled me to come out with my own.

I don't know where I got my copy of *The Mysterious Disappearance of the Marquise of Loria*. I only know that the books with black covers published by Seix Barral's Bilblioteca Breve series always seemed suspicious and thus magnetic to me, even when they lived up to the series title and were as brief as this one. What was suspicious about this particular book? Its long title, perhaps, and the back-cover description announcing the novel as a more or less minor work of the erotic picaresque genre, masterfully written by one of those most suspect of men: a writer of the Latin American Boom. Everyone knows that 100 percent erotic literature — that is, literature written to excite — can only be written from inside the dark workshops of our closets. That's why Lemebel, who wrote from the street, did not write erotic literature but something quite different. Donoso, however, did.

I must have been fourteen or fifteen years old when I first read *The Marquise of Loria*. I would read it many more times, countless when it came to my favorite parts — for example, the scene when Mamerto Sosa, the marquise's hired notary, with his "mothball smell" and his "small but indomitable horn," suddenly falls quiet, "as if . . ." That is, he dies during copulation, after feeling the marquise "squeezing him with a short and violent orgasm." Oh, the moment when Mamerto slowly falls, "as empty and shapeless as a lightweight nightshirt." I know that all of the sex scenes I've written in my life originated here.

Today, as I write this, I'm still holding the same volume from my teenage years, well worn from use, its black skin cracked by damp, the pages dyed sepia from dust and neglect. A life story only has room for a few books with which one truly cohabitates, as with a husband or a lover (or two, or three, or four). That's what the *Marquesita* is on my bookshelf. I'd even say it smells like me. It was my forbidden book, my secret read. I turned to it when I was alone; it came immediately to mind when I heard the rest of my family go out the front door, and if they didn't go out I'd find a way to lock myself in the bathroom with Donoso. Do I belong to the last generation to have masturbated to books? Maybe, but I'm not nostalgic; I have no doubt that these days some people masturbate to social media posts. Reading can still be eroticized.

Rereading today, I can recognize the parts that made me quiver, the passages where I paused to compulsively go over the same lines again and again. Ever faster, ever more urgently, a tightrope walk between culture and pleasure, one hand inside myself and the other in the book, until I came to an end. But the book was endless. I had to wipe it with toilet paper after reading it, and it wasn't exactly tears I was cleaning off. The cover wasn't pink and the prose wasn't purple, and it didn't have a tattletale image on the cover like the books published by La Sonrisa Vertical (The Vertical Smile, an imprint of Tusquets Editores). It wasn't arrogant or blatant. It wasn't performative or pompous. It was a book with a discrete cover, perfect for teenage girls who still lived in all the closets, both figuratively and literally, and were happy there, only there. It could have been mistaken for a YA novel. I liked to think that no one knew my secret, that while my mother was reading feminism for the first time and my father was reading Marx for the umpteenth time, I was cultivating a new genre that augured my future not so much in autofiction as in autoeroticism.

A few years ago I was one of a group of writers asked to choose five objects to form a sort of personal museum inside a suitcase, part of a larger exhibit that would be shown at book fairs. Along with other well-loved objects, including my dead father's broken eyeglasses and a photo of my mother as a child with a shotgun, I chose my copy of the *Marquesita*.

Donoso's "little book" (people always refer to it in the diminutive — oh, how little they know), has more than enough merit to figure in my top five of all time. Because while the patriarchy was keeping me away from Anaïs Nin and Marguerite Duras, before I discovered porn and postporn, before Paul B. Preciado, long before I cut my teeth writing the sexual horoscope for a Spanish magazine marketed to dirty-minded men, before the columns, articles, and books about the body and desire that put food on my table, I embarked upon sex with myself — put this way, I feel my words impregnated with a Donosian erotic flow — in the most cultured way possible: touching myself as I read about this insatiable character's adventures. For me, the Little Marquise was my first porno, my first dildo, and my first love.

José Donoso published the book in 1980, in one of his many times of exile between periods spent Chile. He had already depicted his own social class in *Coronation*, and had shown to the world, maybe not who he was, but at least what he was capable of, in *Hell Has No Limits*, which Arturo Ripstein made into a movie. It had been a decade since *The Obscene Bird of Night* had made him into the best writer in Chile, and one of the best in the Western canon. By then he was married, had adopted a Spanish daughter, and regularly attended dinner parties in Barcelona with the other Boom writers, whose wives had to endure their hours of conversation while laughing at all their jokes. They all felt omnipotent and immortal then, capable of making equally deft incursions into the total novel and the short story, in Santiago, Lima, or Paris, into the Nobel Prize and *clochardismo*, into dramaturgy and politics, into public office and erotic little novels. Universal masters, they set out to include eroticism in great literature, but not to write great erotic literature, which Vargas Llosa once declared nonexistent. But of course it *does* exist, though not everyone gets it right. I'm not here to establish hierarchies—that compulsion is so twentieth century—but I will go to the mat for the potential greatness of genre literature: for me, while neither *Memories of My Melancholy Whores* (Márquez) or *The Bad Girl* (Vargas Llosa) can today be considered great erotic literature, the transgressive and far less well-known antics of the *Marquise of Loria* can. As always, the betrayal starts with a deviation from tradition. Starting from the book's title, we are prepared to be titillated and to jealously guard our secret pleasure, as with any story that's billed as licentious, with all of that genre's most endearing cliches and predictable ingredients, including mystery, death, and games of seduction. But it's all leading us toward an entanglement on another plane of reality that is much more Donosian than excitatory— a phantasmagoric and audacious plane that is very far removed from any pink-covered bodice ripper.

On her way to becoming a full-fledged European, Blanca, a young Nicaraguan woman and the daughter of Latin American diplomats stationed in Madrid, marries Paquito, the young marquess of Loria, but his sudden death from pneumonia makes her into an almost instantaneous and providential widow. As in other works of the genre, we have the premise of a young and attractive woman who, at her husband's death, is consumed by her unusual appetites and iconoclastic spirit, seemingly in permanent revolution.

Donoso also presents Blanca as a woman with white skin, because canonical desire has always been white, and white the normative body. Still, there are constant allusions to Blanca's condition as an immigrant and to her cultural difference, her concern with wealth in the face of European squandering and wastefulness. The marquise's gaze looks from the South to the North, with all the mischievousness and tender mockery of those who, from below, look upon those above.

Though the novel's structure could be called classic, Blanca's tour de force is much more complex than any story in the *Decameron*, and Donoso's imagery is closer to the Marquis de Sade's. To start with, everything we learn about the marquise passes through a filter of humor, satire, and even ridicule. That, too, is a feature of canonical erotic literature as well as the literature of the closet: saying things as if you didn't mean them, hiding behind the curtains of irony and mannered language. But Donoso manages to ironize the very rhetoric of the excitatory text. Not for a second does he neglect his corrosive critique of elites, and it only makes the joke more enduring. I know I'm still laughing. I've been laughing for thirty years. And the irony can turn bitter and thoughtful at times, as it does in Donoso's *Sacred Families: Three Novellas* or in *The Obscene Bird* itself. This Chilean author will take his little marquise through an endless festival of desire and experimentation, and in this erotic-thanatological tour, his character will raze bodies, inhibitions, norms, genders, binaries, and speciesisms. From her early obsession with her callow husband's prominent but not so lively member, through a variety of solitary mystical raptures and successive, perverse rituals where bodies are consumed—from the most honorable to the most libertine, from the tenderest to the most decrepit—all the way to her transpersonal encounter with a ravaging dog "who seemed to offer something more," the little marquise will reveal a search not for *what* but for *whom*, and not only for others, but also for the self; not only for the body but for the *being*. Until the memorable and disorienting final twist that ungenres the novel and definitively hurls the book from the pigeonhole of the great, magnificent little genre novel into a territory that is much less defined, but transcendent.

Just who is our dear little marquise looking for along the tricky pathways of desire? Herself, as the saying goes? But is that self the one that others see, or the elusive one reflected in the mirror, the one who chops off her hair to finally become herself? Is she really a woman? Is she a body, or all bodies? Is she flesh and blood, or is she, not at the end but from the very beginning, a ghost who crosses some ineffable threshold of our desire only to dissolve back into the mist from which there is no return? Is she the delicious fictional object of lust and the vessel for all of one man's fantasies — or all of humanity's? Or even of all the living beings on earth?

I imagine José Donoso creating the little marquise the way the Spanish director Pedro Almodóvar created his dozens of feminine characters, his "Almodóvar girls": exaggerating them, pushing them to the edge, turning them into trans women, into transmutations of their own still lives. Making them into the women he could only dream of being, but whom he loved because they taught him to dream: mothers, daughters, lovers, friends, transvestites smeared with eyeliner, shitty sex, and impossible love.

Some years ago, when Pedro Lemebel was still alive, I interviewed him after he won the José Donoso Prize. I asked if something had to have changed for him, an extravagant queen, to win a prize named after a man who had lived his homosexuality in painful silence. "I don't know that Donoso really did live his homosexuality in painful silence, as you put it," Lemebel replied, "or just in a comfortable closet." I think we can allow ourselves this uncertainty. Pedro was right when he said that Donoso was "a fossil of the bourgeoisie" who didn't have much in common with his own "queer and carnivalesque martyrdom," but precisely because of the contrast, their writings and lives speak to us of the tensions between high and low, between inside and out, between silence and outcry in the writing of diversity and dissidence in Latin America — which always involves pain and blood.

The little marquise of Loria is a Donoso girl. The girl that Donoso never was and always wanted to be, and, just maybe, actually was and always will be. I also wanted to be a Donoso girl, a little clever, just a little silly, a little saintly, a little slutty. At some point I figured out how to create my own character and put it out into the world, but only because others like Donoso and Lemebel taught me to do it, whether behind closed doors or out on the church's front steps. Another instance of literary art's applied beauty: it teaches us to be someone else, and to feel that we are always this person, and others, and others still. I love the marquise because I can be her the way I can both be and not be Madame Bovary or Anaïs Nin, I can be the person I was and that other who desires yet another. And here we come to the twist of the falsely masturbatory little novel: the mysterious occurrence of getting off to good literature, fantastic or existential. Or its flirtation with death, with Bataille or Foucault. And how all this is taking place in Donoso's imagination, opening his closets full of colorful disguises for us, but also contradictions he suffered, unresolved conflicts, and fears and anxieties worn on his sleeve. Forget that he once wrote a letter to his bride telling her how he "was moved to his marrow" when he saw two men showing their love, and felt "envy, desperation," "a desire to have exactly" what those two had, and at the same time "a vehement wish not to be like them," a "terrible temptation" that he admitted hurt just as much or more to realize as to not. Forget that he referred to this as his "primary problem." Forget that he admitted he didn't know where it came from, why it existed, what it meant. Forget that he referred to the desire and love for others like himself as "homosexual envy." Like the lemon-eyed dog devouring him, Donoso seemed to see his own "alabaster body stained with bruises and welts, striped with scratches, clearly marked by the beast's fangs, making [him] into a sort of tenebristic, *tremendista*, and tragic saint, a horrific and bloody martyr." Like the queer Lemebelian martyr.

And that's why it's a pleasure to see him like this, dressed as the little marquise, being the marquise of Donoso, trying out everything: homosexuality, threesomes, polyamory, scatology, interspecies love. And how can these images not remind us of his daughter Pilar, writing, publishing to acclaim, freeing herself from the paternal yoke and, simultaneously, dying. And freeing him as well.

Sometimes I have the unsettling feeling that my life, and as such my writing, are the product of a queer Chilean man's fevered imagination. I even live in Madrid. I had forgotten that the novel is set in the city that has sheltered me for over a decade now. I just remembered it now, in these recent days of nostalgic rereading, as I've gotten turned on again and walked down the same streets the marquise walks, the areas around Casa de Campo and Puerta de Hierro. And I've gone to Retiro Park and thought I saw the little marquise beside her dark, wild, pale-eyed dog, like a mutant, solitary, savage creature, showing me the way out of this gray labyrinth.

— GABRIELA WEINER

THE MYSTERIOUS DISAPPEARANCE
OF THE MARQUISE OF LORIA

THE YOUNG MARQUISE, WIDOW OF LORIA, BORN BLANCA
Arias in Managua, Nicaragua, was the typical daughter of Latin American diplomats—the kind who, after a stint in Madrid as brief as it was
empty, leave no other evidence of their passage through the capital
than a pretty daughter married into a title. When the exotic regime
that had exported Arias fell, he found himself obliged to return to the
homeland that had elevated him so fleetingly, where he was to fulfill
one more chapter of his dark destiny.

Blanca dried the tears so copiously shed the moment she was sev-
ered from her family—for, as the oldest and loveliest, she had always
been very pampered. Still, it wasn't long after her parents' departure
before she was a full-fledged European, replacing those innocent at-
tachments with others, and forgetting both the luscious intonations of
her native vernacular and the liberties that were current among girls
on the young continent in order to wrap herself in the sumptuous
mantle of all the prejudices, rituals, and diction of her brand-new
rank. These, Blanca knew despite her scant nineteen years, involved
nothing more than a change of clothes; ultimately, it had all been as
easy as throwing off an embroidered *huipil* in favor of a Paul Poiret
tunic—a garment that made it easy to exercise other liberties that, as
long as she kept to certain rules, every civilized lady—which is what
she now was—has the right to exercise.

Blanca relished preparing for just such exercises under the carapace
of the elegant but extremely strict mourning that, for the moment,

would not even allow for satin trimming or bias-cut silk. Mourning granted her a sort of moratorium: from the bastion of her splendid widowhood, protected by the barred windows of her palazzo, she could gaze out at the horizon and wisely choose that which could offer her the most pleasure. She was young, she was rich, she was beautiful: she had plenty of time to do things well. And while she languidly prepared to do just that, no intrusive eye, not even that of the mother marquise, had access to her private *fraise écrasée*–colored bedchamber to spy on her as she surrendered to vague reveries and caresses practiced since childhood as an exercise of her own freedom, as affirmation and enjoyment of the same. Those romps had continued — without ceasing to be, in essence, what they had always been — throughout the five months of her marriage to the opulent but unskilled marquess of Loria, lamentably felled by a case of diphtheria caught as he left a rainy carnival dance that he attended recklessly disguised as Icarus.

Blanca had never known a man besides him. After leaving the convent school where she was educated, she went almost directly to the altar. But it would be imprecise to say that it was merely her five months of marriage — as one would presume, due to her careful education, imparted as much by the black women of the tropics as by the Spanish nuns — that brought out appetites previously unknown in her: to be rigorous, we'd have to admit that Blanca had played with these appetites her whole life, in the company of cousins and little girlfriends, most especially during the torrid siestas of vacations spent in spacious old mansions on her relatives' Caribbean properties. However, she never got the wrong idea, and never forgot that she was only practicing for the real thing: the future held plenitude in store for her, no doubt about it, for she never questioned her own beauty, and being beautiful, she knew full well, meant she was entitled to the very best of everything. Before her marriage, she'd been a child. Those five months, one way or another, made her into a woman. But not because Paquito Loria turned out to be a skillful lover: skinny, pale, with transparent skin that emphasized his sunken eyes, he possessed, nevertheless, the sinful fantasies born of draining himself alone night after night in his bed at a Catholic boarding school.

At the dance where the happy couple first met, during a perhaps calculatedly clumsy moment of the cakewalk, Blanca suddenly became aware of attributes as well-proportioned as they were ferrous in the thus far extremely dull marquess. No doubt it was the satin of her pretty creole arms or the lightness of her uncorseted waist, which the boy's hands palpated between folds of slippery silk, that put Paquito's qualities on full display. And Blanca, for her part, realizing during the second foxtrot that the marquess's attributes had grown to the point that they were surely unsurpassable, said to herself:

"It's what I've dreamed of my whole life."

Sliding into the next foxtrot, open-mouthed in admiration as if before a monument, and avid as if contemplating an artwork, Blanca concluded:

"I want him for myself."

It didn't take much work to get him. Like Blanca, Paquito was fresh out of high school, and the stem of this exotic flower that gave off such unsettling perfume was, all told, the first thing other than himself that his eager hands encountered. His mother, the widow marquise, was an imposing lady of nearly forty years old. She spent some of her winters in Paris and spoke French with a Sevillian accent—and Spanish, to be sure, with a French accent. As is only natural, she tried to oppose this insignificant marriage of her idiot son, who now boasted the title and could realize at any moment that it was his right to dispose of the House of Loria's substantial fortune in any way he pleased. As for the widow, her husband had bequeathed to her—and this was only one more of his cowardly acts of revenge—a pension that, without mincing words, was rubbish.

During the young marquess's visits to the apartment of the welcoming diplomats, who didn't realize they were in danger of losing a daughter—or else were resigned to the loss, given that they had four other beauties to marry off—Blanca waged her elemental battle in the

5

Turkish corner of the Residence, atop a sofa brimming with cushions, the censer exuding an aroma of musk. Obstructed by bodices that shielded anxious breasts, by starched shirts that cracked with the discomfort of certain effusions, by piqué vests that scratched in a moment of passion, by spat buttons tangled in lace when the lovers' mouths sank into one another's anatomies, and poorly disguised by the latest issue of *La Esfera* or the volume of stories by Hoyos y Vinent in which they feigned interest so as to throw off Blanca's parents or her envious and nosy little sisters, millimeter by millimeter they versed themselves in their mutual topographies so sweaty with fear and desire, the hot vapor of their vegetative hollows, their crevices and protuberances swollen with love, while their gluttonous mouths, never satisfied, were filled again and again with the other's fragrant flesh. Consoling each other over circumstances so unpropitious to going any further, they told themselves it was all a stupendous simulacrum, so that when the moment came for total love to pierce them, so much practice could only enhance what would doubtless be an astonishing reward.

As his beloved's birthday drew near, Paquito begged his mother to bestow a courtesy upon his friend Blanca Arias. "But heavens, what sort of courtesy?" the dowager marquess exclaimed. She did not know those people. She had given them her gloved hand only once, when Paquito introduced her to the entire family—Casilda Loria didn't stammer when, asked by her son for her opinion afterwards, she labeled them *unbearable*—during a benefit jazz lunch at the Palace. What was her son demanding of her? Wasn't it enough to send a bouquet of flowers, a box of violet candies?

What else could she do, when she was not inclined to get involved with such people?

"You can invite them to our box at the Royal Theater."

Casilda Loria, annoyed at this use of the possessive which her son was employing for the first time and clearly as a means of coercion, directed her reply not to him, but to her great and good friend the count of Almanza, a sportsman who was related to the house by a vague Andalusian line, and who boasted a thick handlebar mustache similar to that of the prize-winning poet Don Eduardo Marquina:

"Don't you think it's a tragedy to have such an out-and-out imbecile for a son? Do you think it fair that, being the most self-sacrificing of mothers, as I have been, Paquito should demand I make a spectacle of myself on a night of the Royal's season by appearing with a fat lady gussied up like a tavern cook on Palm Sunday? And him, all shiny and black like a grand piano? What's more, that night they're performing *Lohengrin*, a difficult opera, and, I must confess, a somewhat boring one, which they will certainly be unable to appreciate. I simply don't understand where that girl got her fair skin, her beauty . . ."

"Oh! So you admit it, then . . . ?"

Casilda didn't like to speak directly to Paquito, who, according to her, was cold as unbaked dough and had a permanent odor of boarding-school breakfast on his breath: she left him with the question on his lips and went out with Almanza to take a spin in the new Isotta Fraschini.

Descending the marble steps of the palazzo — which was in danger of ending up in the hands of that little upstart of a girl — as the sun filtering through the stained-glass herons in the windows shifted the colors of her stylized face, attentive, as usual, to her friend's wise advice, Casilda gradually came over to his side: she shouldn't be silly, Almanza said, at the end of the day it was Paquito's pennies, now he was of age, that paid for the new car and the Italian driver with his cap and spats. Luckily, Paquito was utterly stupid, and, if he got married, he would be absorbed with Blanca for a long time — the count used the vulgar term "pussy-crazed" and the haughty marquise didn't bat an eyelash — so that it would be a good while before he took an interest in inquiring of Don Mamerto Sosa, the notary who had always taken care of the Lorias' matters and who tended to be somewhat difficult, just who had the legal right to open and close the family purse. They had plenty of time to look for solutions. Casilda shouldn't worry. Furthermore, Blanca was alone, or nearly so, because, given the fragility of American political regimes, her parents would soon be gone, leaving no one to look out for her. How dangerous it would be, on the other hand, if Paquito got it into his head to fall in love with one of Pepe Manzanares's seven daughters, for example — Pepe had the capital and yields of all the fortunes of the Spanish nobility at his fingertips! She should let the kids have their fun, the count declared. They would have plenty of time to pull one over on that idiot Don Mamerto and get him to put everything at their disposal, long before the boy ever wised up. In any case, for now, if Casilda preferred not to appear in public with those insignificant diplomats, it was very easy to arrange things so the audience of the Royal Theater would know they were guests of Paquito's — he was plenty old enough to manage such commitments — and not hers: Almanza, personally, would see to it that pink champagne of the sweetest variety was brought at the opportune time. For now, that was enough. Later, of course, would come the bitter pill of the wedding itself. He wasn't suggesting it would be easy to neutralize these people who seemed to have only recently climbed down from the trees. But why get ahead of themselves?

"Where *could* that girl have gotten such beauty . . . ?" mused the count of Almanza, and, spreading his fur shawl over the widow marquise's knees as well as his own, he tapped on the window separating them from the driver to signal they were ready to start off.

"Her mother is clearly a hussy, though retired," Casilda opined. "The girl must be the daughter of some drunken U.S. marine passing through a Caribbean port . . ."

The night of the invitation, the marquise of Loria received the diplomat, his wife, and their daughter in the anteroom of the family's box, where no one could see them. Yes, Casilda said to herself, the girl was superb and would pass muster anywhere, with her big, round eyes like a lively monkey's, her pursed, succulent lips, her strong, wet, alabaster teeth. Her toned arms, as if carved by a master, sprung forth from the perfection of secretive armpits just barely revealed by the cut of her plunging, sleeveless dress. Her legs were a pinch short, though. She was, however, a fresh and fragrant little animal who would give her son plenty of work, though her somewhat *potelée* figure — which time and easy living would exacerbate—would never be truly chic. The kid had good taste. Inherited, of course, from his mother: one had only to look at Almanza.

As soon as the lights went down and the prelude of the first act began, Casilda invited the two older Ariases to settle in beside her in the box's front row. Blanca sat behind her mother, and behind Blanca, perched on his seat and leaning his forearm on his beloved's backrest, Paquito pointed out this and that in the program. In the darkest back corner of the box, the count of Almanza plopped down, growling that he planned to nap: he detested Wagner—all that shouting, and in German to boot.

When the curtain rose on a forest clearing beside a river in Brabant, Paquito leaned toward Blanca's ear to explain in a low voice what was happening onstage: Ortrud and Telramund were very bad, which is clear from the start even though Ortrud didn't open her mouth in the whole first act, and Elsa, because she was lovely and dressed in white, was very good, and she hoped for a knight to come and defend her honor against the accusations of her perverse aunt and uncle in a Trial by Combat. Beside the marquess's lips, his lover's ear was snowy, barely pinkish, like the most delicate of buds, and, as he spoke, he couldn't resist the temptation to risk a kiss on its lobe. Ortrud stood up with a furious look, but since her rage had not been provoked by Paquito's kiss, which no one could see—Casilda was too concerned with hiding her face behind a fan; the diplomat's wife too entranced with Elsa's diamonds, which, as Almanza had recently informed her, were a gift from a well-known conservative politician; and the minister was too busy gloating over the shine of his medals—Paquito ventured to touch, with just the tip of his tongue, that labyrinth of cool flesh that soon grew warm, his taste buds receiving the shudder with which Blanca welcomed his caress: because he knew her, the marquess was sure that nothing, not even the blink of an eye, would betray her pleasure. With the hand that wasn't holding the program, hidden between the golden chair and the partition between the boxes, he caressed, first, the ribs of his beloved's backrest, then downward, to the seat, and there, after resting a few anguished seconds on the garnet silk, he inserted it—very gently—between the seat and Blanca's sublime rear end. Discovering that, as if she were expecting it, she didn't even flinch, he fondled and groped the mysterious inlet that separated her buttocks. But his fingertips, eager for living flesh, slowly rounded the hip, sliding, then, over the *satin duchesse* of the dress covering the length of her amenable thigh. More than amenable, Paquito could tell: Blanca pressed that thigh against his hand, offering him the tender little animal that awaited him huddled between one thigh and the other, there in the depths he needed to reach while the arias of incomparable love came one after the other onstage. He had only to attain the hem of her very short skirt. Without moving, without shifting the attention of his half-smiling face as it reflected the luminous details onstage, Paquito extended his arm a little more, feeling his beloved shiver as she caught his hand with her knee, and even further as he delved into the hot curve where she trapped the hand by bending her leg and pressing it with her calf. Synchronizing this passionate, secret movement with an elegant public one, Blanca took the program that Paquito was holding in his free hand, and, after briefly studying it, let it fall open onto her lap to shield the marquess's hand as it quite audaciously probed under her dress, passing the garter and finally reaching the longed-for skin of the thigh, only to press on even higher, into that first vegetation, where he paused his caress. He would go no further, he told himself: let Blanca, driven to distraction, beg him, demand, with a movement of her thigh, that he progress onward to the exquisite goal. At the moment of the swan's arrival on the cardboard water, Casilda looked proudly—as if she owned of every one of those props—over at Blanca. She discovered such concentration on that face so ignorant of refinement that she could only muse on how some very primitive beings—this lovely girl, for example—are so pure that they are granted comprehension of the most inaccessible and exclusive of the arts. She and Almanza excused themselves before the first act ended, for they had promised to go and play a few hands of ombre in the anteroom of his cousin,

Teresa Castillo, who would be offended unto death if they left her alone during act two, which was terribly boring: they would rather play cards. They'd return toward the end of the act.

When they came back and took their seats, Casilda saw a pair of young profiles so absorbed in the tragic results of Elsa's blunder that they shot her only the briefest smiles of welcome. As soon as the marquise was settled, the two profiles were once again as motionless as those of an imperial couple stamped on a coin. Casilda sighed: she was no longer young. She had seen too much opera in her lifetime, and she was a bit blasé by now, so that while Blanca Arias's musical ecstasy moved her in its naivete, she also found it exasperatingly American. Almanza, emerging from the anteroom just before the curtain fell, informed them that the champagne was ready. Casilda ushered her guests through just before the lights came on and people started turning their opera glasses upward to see who was visiting the boxes of whom.

The conversation in Casilda Loria's antechamber on this occasion was extremely animated: the minister's wife never tired of admiring Elsa's long blonde braids, and made sure everyone knew that she, in her homeland, had cousins with hair every bit as long and blond as the soprano's—and with blue eyes, no less! Almanza didn't deem it necessary to burst her bubble by informing her that in this case the hair was a wig, because while La Velásquez *was* lovely, her hair was as black as a crow's wing. And he should know, for he had been acquainted with her since her modest beginnings, because, like him, she was from Huelva, and he could hear her Andalusian accent and the trill of the fandango even when she was singing in German. Paquito, meanwhile, loquacious as never before, relayed what had occurred onstage to His Excellency, who hadn't understood a thing. As he spoke, the young marquess brought the fingers of his left hand to his nose and sniffed them, peering at Blanca out of the corner of his eye. Not missing a thing, Blanca struggled to keep from laughing, but allowed a few charming dimples to bloom in her cheeks. Irritated at Paquito's gesture, Casilda scolded him:

"Please refrain from picking your nose in the presence of your friends. How is it possible that you're twenty years old and still haven't lost your schoolboy manners?"

Paquito kept a gloomy silence after that, drinking glass after glass of champagne, restless because, though the performance was five minutes into its final act, they still hadn't taken their seats in the box. When they finally returned to their places, Blanca rolled the program into a tube. She held it erect and caressed it tenderly, repeatedly, with her other hand, from top to bottom and bottom to top. Paquito's left hand, anxious not to lose the precious time they had left before the show was over, was already probing between Blanca's eagerly separated thighs into that viscous bud whose pistil he was trying to drive mad. Understanding the suggestion of the upright program, he sought himself out with his free hand, dreaming that the caress Blanca was lavishing on the pamphlet was actually being lavished upon him, to thus reach a rapture of love that paralleled Elsa and Lohengrin's on the shores of the Brabante river. Now. Right now. It was a question of prolonging the passionate duet for a few more minutes, because the swan had yet to arrive . . .

When the tenor started into "In Fernen Land . . . ," Paquito and Blanca, tense, close to ecstasy, panting, nevertheless remained nearly still, because any movement could give them away and prevent them from reaching their pinnacle. She kept her face fixed, shining with the lights of the scenic drama, but in secret she rocked her hips, the sweet lower part of her body submerged in darkness and sticking to the silk of her dress and the seat, while keeping her torso perfectly motionless. From the back of the box, the count of Almanza watched their calisthenics, as furtive as they were efficient, with unspeakable ecstasy. He hadn't missed a single gesture, not one movement, not a second of the tender dalliance of those two doves, remembering, not without a measure of nostalgia, how something not so different — taking into consideration the difficulties presented by the feminine attire of fifteen years prior — had happened with Casilda in this very box, in the presence of her blind fool of a husband: the opera was *La Juive*, he recalled, by Halévy. Enraptured, rejuvenated by the young couple's subtle but maddening rhythm that became more and more frenetic as the sweaty demands of love intensified onstage, the count joined in with the exquisite Blanca, with Paquito, with the music that transported them in their eloquent sensuality, which he was following closely and participating in.

At the moment when the tenor reveals that he is the son of Parsifal and the ballad concludes with a *tutti* from the orchestra, Blanca, Paquito, and Almanza shuddered in unison. Blanca, with her eyelids half-closed, sank into such a soft moan of ecstasy that the dowager marquise looked over at her: these people! she thought. But when she saw Blanca's pretty face in such a profound rapture of artistic emotion during that instant of sublime music, she felt quite edified. Fearing a fainting spell, she started to offer Blanca her jar of smelling salts, but then she saw that the girl was fanning herself with her program without taking her eyes from the stage, which seemed sufficient to restore her. For the last time before leaving, Casilda ran her eyes over the theater. Paquito used this moment of his mother's divided attention to button himself up again. Almanza followed his lead, also quickly, because he'd recognized Casilda's characteristic movements as she gathered up handkerchief, glasses, and purse before leaving.

The marquise of Loria stood up. Feigning a true terror of crowds due to her asthma, she summarily—though affably, so her son would have nothing to reproach her for if things progressed—took her leave of the guests, whispering that she didn't want to ruin the end of the opera for them. And as he placed the sumptuous *petit-gris* stole over Casilda's shoulders in the anteroom, the count of Almanza heard her murmur, half to him, half reflecting to herself:

"That girl is really *quite* sensitive to music . . ."

"*Quite* . . ." agreed the count.

And, taking his great and good friend by the arm, they went together, as so many times before, down the Royal Theater's marble steps—a little pensive this time, though they didn't know why—and left Paquito, who was a big boy now, to take care of the guests.

2

THE LESS SAID ABOUT THE WEDDING ITSELF, THE BETTER.
Casilda, vanquished by her son's irrepressible passion and by Almanza's logic, used the regrettable death of a great-aunt who was mother
superior at a convent of the order of Saint Claire in Málaga—whom
she hadn't seen since the woman was her confirmation sponsor—as
an excuse to celebrate the ceremony in strict privacy. So private that
Blanca and Paquito were married in the remote village of Alarcón de
los Arcos, a fief of the Lorias since time immemorial, in the ruinous
church filled with locals—the only beings on the face of the earth,
according to Almanza, geographically required to take a twit like
Paquito seriously merely because of his lineage. The banquet—if
such a rustic feast can even qualify as such—was held in the leaky,
blazon-filled manse that no one—except maybe some adventurous
administrator sent by Don Mamerto Sosa, Casilda supposed—had
visited in fifteen years. Aside from the Sosa family, who hailed from
that one-horse town, plus the little group of intimate friends Casilda
and Almanza met up with to play bridge—so they could at least have
someone to laugh with as they discussed the event afterwards—and
the staff of the consulate, which turned out to be an army, the event
was attended only by the five or six people who constituted the local
Nicaraguan community: the men, impressed even by the mold on all
those antiques; the women, tarted up—as was to be expected—as
though for a Palace ball.

Marriage, in its strictest sense, was a cruel disappointment for

Blanca: anything that involved playfulness, touching, lips, laughter, tickling, caresses, had all been stupendous because it had been imaginative, audacious, because Paquito refused any limits to pleasure as long as it was formulated in terms of a perverse romp. But night after long and silent night in the large private bedroom they occupied in the palazzo—once her son's marriage forced Casilda to move out—the marquess fell, defeated, just when his mettle was about to satisfy her appetite: it was as if all of Paquito's iron melted right at the peak of desire, wetting only the outside of the admirable flower of flesh that Blanca offered him so unproblematically.

"Darling, my darling . . ." she consoled Paquito, reassuring him that the things they did were what she most liked, and since they had their whole lives ahead of them for the other thing, for now it was best to enjoy this—which was, she assured him, quite something.

To Paquito, too long was the night, and too large the bedroom that had so recently belonged to his mother—who, upon withdrawing, declared that she was unwilling to play the role of a freeloading relative in her own house. Nevertheless, she used the palazzo as an outpost of her own extremely modern apartment, receiving guests and giving orders there as if she, and not Blanca, were its mistress. The silence of that great house was too respectful, claimed Paquito, and the baldachin could fall on top of them any minute, he added, made ever more neurotic by his failures as the weeks went by. Blanca, in spite of protests from Casilda—who abandoned her relative discretion to object to the American girl's audacity in daring to question her taste in interior design—had the baldachin taken away, the bed moved to a more intimate corner, and a large mirror hung on the wall across from the bed. All of it useless.

"My darling . . . don't cry . . ." she went on consoling him in an attempt to stanch his rage.

In appreciation of his wife's tenderness, Paquito went back on the attack, his love and pride solidly reconstituted: he was capable of anything with his fingers, his knee, with his eager and daring lips, even with his prominent nose if necessary. Blessed as she was with that stunning vocation for naughtiness that tends to come hand-in-hand with the tenderness of females from the tropics, Blanca laughed and accepted and loved, not without longing, it's true, for the definitive thing, but for the definitive thing *with Paquito,* because during the five months that her marriage lasted, Blanca never dreamed of other men, as she had before and would later. She was very beautiful—truly, more beautiful since her marriage than before it. Because she knew this, she felt capable of anything, too, even of reviving Paquito after his floundering night after exasperating night. She knew it would take time. But her feminine instinct assured her heart that maybe it wouldn't be so very long before Paquito, stimulated by her beauty, would enter triumphantly—and, so to speak, through the front door—to occupy the throne she had designated for him within her body.

After studying her husband and his repeated failures with a fair amount of detachment but the greatest possible tenderness, she established a sort of gradual strategy that would, she thought, ensure her triumph. She soon reached the conclusion that what most bothered him in the amplitude of the silent, palatial, conjugal night was the absence of the forbidden, the accidental, the ambush, the threatening footsteps drawing near or doors creaking open at just the wrong moment, evoking censure, punishment, shame—all essential elements, according to Blanca, for the maintenance of her husband's complicated vigor, so different from the American simplicity of her own—until the moment he could strike to the fullest. But wasn't it impossible to produce startling situations in a marriage as conventional as theirs, with a much more than comfortable economic position? Artifice: that was the solution Blanca reached. And since she was determined as well as intelligent and enamored, once she managed to isolate the missing pieces, she set out to procure them for the young marquess.

It would be too tedious to describe the occasions on which Blanca, by means of her perhaps overly transparent stagings of danger, was on the verge of knowing happiness. But we cannot omit one memorable afternoon when they almost reached the culmination: Casilda and

Almanza had summoned Tere Castillo and Pepe Manzanares, who were entangled at the time, to play bridge at the palazzo in a corner of the graceful salon with its large French Renaissance fireplace. On the other side of the three-person sofa and the Boulle lamps and tables loaded with showy frames and pricey knickknacks, Blanca and Paquito lounged on cushions in front of the happy fire in the hearth which, from time to time, overcoming their languor, they fed with another pine cone or two. Blanca had been caressing Paquito's head for a long time, while he, lazily, lovingly, tormented his wife's vulnerable little nipples under her blouse. Around the bridge table, the elders occasionally broke the long silences of their sterile concentration with laughter, but, so near his family — to him, the source of all punishment — Paquito was inflamed. Blanca unbuttoned her husband's pants, and he emerged, reddened from reflected fire and his own candescence, hard from danger and the dampness of Blanca's kisses. They saw Almanza stand up because he was the dummy that round. He only had to turn his head and he would catch the young couple in the act.

"Now . . ." whispered Paquito, startled but ready as soon as he perceived the danger.

And since she never wore undergarments so she'd be ready for exactly such an occasion as this, Blanca lifted her short skirt and climbed astride her husband. The little marquise's pretty eyes — as she sat atop her husband's body, her face was level with the tabletops and the backrests of the armchairs and sofas — found Almanza's gaze, as for a while now he'd been spying on the couple out of the corner of his eye. When she felt that beneath her, Paquito was starting to falter from a lack of external stimulation, the girl's expressive gaze implored the gentleman for help: that he — who was reputed to have done it all in his life, including fritter away his wealth on that chanteuse from Cadiz that he'd kept at the Hotel Negresco, so that, by all accounts, he now had to live at Casilda's expense (or rather Paquito's) — yes, that he should give her this chance to experience the heretofore unknown fullness, yes, that's what the marquise's pretty, mischievous eyes were imploring of him. The count, a worldly gentleman to the core, expert in decoding women's mute pleas, this time understood as well that the message carried a postscript: the promise that later, between the two of them, they would settle accounts. Almanza went over to the phonograph in the center of the room, halfway between the bridge table and the fireplace, and started to wind it up.

"Careful, my darling, Almanza is near," Blanca whispered, leaning closer to the ear of her passionately fluttering husband—for, with that proximity of danger, the poor man could finally feel all his own tension fully inside the tensed ring of Blanca's flesh as it girded him.

At the bridge table, meanwhile, a concentrated silence reigned, leaving the three of them isolated in a different part of the salon, beside the fireplace. Almanza chose a record, put it on the turntable and lowered the needle, which hissed a little before the rhythms of "The Wedding of the Painted Doll" rang out. The count leaned his noble head toward the phonograph's horn as though to hear better, but in reality he wanted to keep the bouquet of yellow chrysanthemums in their Lalique vase from impeding his participation in the pleasure of the couple by the fire: Paquito's trunk upright once again, Blanca's eyelids damp with love as she slowly, skillfully sank her light body down over his in a dorsal recumbent position, insinuating, with a very slight push and pull that only the marquess's most sensitive organs could perceive, the rhythm of the foxtrot coming from the gramophone. In order to finally touch bottom and make their delirium complete, Paquito grasped Blanca's buttocks, opening his eyes wide in surprise at his marvelous feat. Unfortunately, just then his eyes happened to meet the permissive gaze of the count, who was disguising his delight behind the chrysanthemums, leaning over the gramophone's horn like the RCA Victor dog. The marquess had only to see that complacence, to feel that complicity, and everything in him suddenly withdrew, collapsing right there when his path to triumph was already lubricated, without even feeling the useless discharge with which he usually soaked Blanca. The count, satisfied because he thought he had fulfilled his mission and as such would be able to charge the young marquise's account in kind, walked away and returned to the bridge table, where the others were commenting on the outcome of the hand.

"With a hand like that," alleged Pepe Manzanares, "I couldn't do a thing."

Paquito buried his face in crossed arms propped on bent knees. When he heard those words from the rotund Pepe, the young marquess couldn't refrain from contradicting him:

"The hand is the only thing that doesn't fail . . ." wailed Paquito, nearly in tears.

"Shhhh . . ." Blanca whispered.

"What a cold you have, son!" Casilda exclaimed without looking up from her hand full of spades, or waiting for a reply to her comment. "Blanca, have you asked if they've brought the wings for Paquito's costume over from the nuns at the convent, where I had them made? Let's have him try them on right away."

"Why, if I'm incapable of flying?"

"Are you going to dress him as Mermoz?" asked Tere Castillo as she tossed an ace of hearts onto the center of the tablecloth. "I certainly don't mean to diminish him in your eyes, but I don't think Paquito has quite the right body type . . ."

"He's going as Icarus," interrupted Almanza. "Though, since he has a cold, I don't even want to think about how an overcoat is going to fit over his tunic and wings."

"It won't be cold tomorrow night," ruled the widow marquise, taking all the spades and hearts from the table. "So Paquito won't go as an eyesore and let his little demigod costume be spoiled by a common overcoat."

Paquito, in effect, did not wear an overcoat. Everyone greatly admired the skill with which pure nunnish hands had dyed and glued the chicken feathers to lend veracity to his wings. But he lost his little crown of glitter-gilded laurels soon after the dance began, and, without it, sticking close to Blanca's skirts because so much commotion made him uneasy, they decided to flee the ball just as it was starting to heat up. Not wanting Casilda to know about their defection, they didn't call for the Isotta Fraschini—that rascal of an Italian driver would be playing cards with the other chauffeurs in one of the cars' back seats, so they decided not to summon him—but instead ran to the taxi stop on the corner. During that short run it started pouring rain, destroying the unlucky marquess's wings, drenched feathers sticking to the wet tunic that clung to his back and thighs, so that he arrived home to the palazzo a shivering, sorry mess. That winter, there was a lot of diphtheria going around Madrid: two days after the Wednesday of the carnival, Francisco Javier Anacleto Quiñones, the marquess of Loria, passed away before his twenty-first year, leaving all of his relatives disconsolate, but especially his young widow—born Blanca Arias, daughter of a notable Nicaraguan diplomat, as the society pages of the newspaper recorded—whose beauty, everyone remarked in the pews of Saint Jerome's, where the funeral procession began, was only emphasized by mourning.

3

FURTIVE . . . OR MORE LIKE SPONTANEOUS AND FRESH?

These were very different, nearly contradictory modes, which she, in her inexperience, had gotten confused. This was what Blanca was thinking about as she strolled through Retiro Park during that first spring of her widowhood, laden with black ribbons, a monkey fur muff protecting her hands. Yes, what Paquito had needed to "fulfill himself," so to speak, was above all *spontaneity* in the act of love, which marriage killed off with its permissiveness, codified and sterilized through schedules and terms. She had committed the stupidity of confusing that longing, which was natural in a pure soul, with a certain child-ishly perverse leaning of his fantasy toward the furtive and forbidden. Since nothing was really forbidden in marriage, she had been misled. She didn't plan to let it happen again. How would she have ended up if Paquito's ideals had been realized? Deep down, very deep, so far down that the impact of this certainty was very slight, barely the brush of a coal-black wing, she thought that it would be almost like exhaustion, old age, the very opposite of this maddening longing for the unknown that drove her to walk, dainty and swaying, around the Crystal Palace, to then pause on the steps to the pond where she could contemplate her own mourning image in the water — like a marvelous black swan among so many white ones — and to enjoy so intensely what she saw reflected there. In spite of the love she still professed for her unforgettable husband, she accepted the inevitable fact that her own destiny would be to experience everything. Which of the plump mestiza servants with colorful kerchiefs around their heads, the ones who'd told her stories of spells in the moonlight beside waters teeming with dangers far greater than these tame swans, could have ever foreseen, in the cards they so loved to read, that her fate was to be deliciously fulfilled in this civilized world where — for the elegant lady life's vicissitudes had turned her into — everything, including disillusionment, was clear and predictable, and thus manageable? And yet, after all these months, she could still feel the sweet burn of the ring that Paquito had fit forever into her flesh to the rhythm of "The Wedding of the Painted Doll" that one and only time when he had fleetingly touched her deepest part. It was as if that seed of sensation, in this accursed springtime when everything was fructifying and filling with juices, was putting down roots through her whole anatomy, animating her entire being, making her more tender and fragrant and on offer.

But on offer, ultimately, to what, to whom . . . ? Gazing at her reflection in the pond, she felt a slight vertigo, as if the tingling roots that sprouted from that frugal memory were so bristling with tactile sensations that her fantasizing body, in this state of synesthesia, was in danger of suffering a fainting spell: she had to turn her back on herself to prevent it. Nevertheless, the exasperating question persisted: to whom, for what? She would never again feel the tender love that she'd felt for her Paquito; but she was constantly unsettled by a sense of certainty that her destiny was to experience all the things spelled out in the black servants' cards, those dealt to her and all the others, too. For the moment, the only creature who could harvest the divine fruits of her ardor was Blanca herself, alone and locked in her bedroom, with the forced reiteration of her one meager memory: this, wallowed in and abused and invoked with moans and sighs between her fragrant sheets as she sought out the mysterious little button of pleasure again and again with fingers well trained in the matter, was gradually worn away from repetition ad nauseam, so much so that now, on her most restless nights, she found it difficult to hold onto. Then she had no other choice but to give terrifying free rein to her fantasies, which left her wet from exhaustion and frustration, as if she'd been raped by a battalion of clumsy adversaries. She didn't dare indulge these fantasies, though she knew the door was wide open to do so: for now she feared everything and everyone, her mother-in-law, her friends, Almanza, Don Mamerto Sosa, his lackeys—all the men and women, in sum, whom she saw coming toward her on the sidewalk, and whose scrutiny of her person pierced the enigmatic chic of her mourning, stripping her of the brooch fastened at her neckline in the crease of her heaving breasts, of the little *crêpe marocain* skirt that the spring breeze adhered to her hips, the curves of which revealed neither slip nor panties, of the little veil that lent the broad, low brim of her hat a subtle shiver; yes, everyone wanted to undress her, to touch her, to caress her skin, to bite her marvelous flesh ... any gesture of hers could give her away, and they could realize that she was in such a state that she would be incapable of refusing anything to anyone who asked. Almanza's hand, for example, clasped hers for half a second longer than was appropriate as they were saying goodbye, and as he kissed it, his waxed mustache carried unmistakable intentions when it brushed her knuckles. Or were those just invented fantasies? It was so hard to say what was and what wasn't ... !

Blanca held a bit of a grudge toward Almanza. She couldn't forget how, on that memorable afternoon beside the fire, Paquito had fallen defeated in the exact instant his ardor was touched by the crude complicity in the count's gaze. That same night, with his poor body as cold as the moon, Paquito had analyzed the recent problem in the light of that contemptible gaze, assigning it the blame for his failure as he lay beside her in their bed reflected by the mirror. The ill-fated wings still yet to be worn hung on the back of a chair: the hope of something that would never be fulfilled.

Paquito, whose Jesuit education had not been in vain, was very given to rumination and analysis. He was far from being the twit others believed him to be, and he had perceived everything from a very young age, in spite of how his family and servants all elided the shameful truth, starting with how Almanza had weaseled his way into the house in full view and knowledge of Paquito's good-natured father, who became the laughingstock of all Madrid, and continuing as the count claimed endless privileges for himself even while the blinded elder marquess was still alive. And now, his unfounded authority in the family had the young marquess fed up. Upon his father's death, Almanza even made an attempt to marry Casilda, a proposition to which she, who was clearly no fool, replied: "A widow who remarries doesn't deserve to be a widow." She rejected from the outset what would have been a very bad business for her, and kept the count on as a kind of poor relation without a fixed allowance, who primarily saw to matters of luxury in the house — the pink champagne for the Arias family, for example.

In any case, his mother and Almanza — and, he suspected, also that cynic Tere Castillo, in some way that he still couldn't understand — lived at his expense, controlling administrators and notaries, servants and relatives, and, ever since he came of age, forcing him to sign endless documents that they didn't even let him read:

"You'll thank me when you're older," Casilda would say.

But all of that was going to end. Yes, it was all going to change starting *tomorrow*, wailed the nude Paquito as he paced so energetically that his large, white, limp member swung like a plumb line. He gave the damned wings a kick. But his aggression went no further than that, since the masked ball that Blanca so longed to attend was to be held tomorrow, and he didn't have the heart to ruin it, deciding instead to postpone the confrontation until the day after.

At the ball, as soon as he donned his Icarus wings, Paquito felt that member, so limp the night before, now rise up invincible, unprecedentedly engorged by his project of putting up a fight against his mother and Almanza as soon as the next day, giving them a real piece of his mind, to which they would listen even if they closed themselves off to everything and declared his actions déclassé: his vigor was sudden, and rather scandalous, for the skimpy classical attire made it impossible to hide a thing. He dragged Blanca away from the ball intending to take her straight to their bedroom, where, for both of their pleasure, he planned to ravish her without even removing his wings, without even giving her time to shed her shepherdess's hoop skirts. This venture had the regrettable outcome that we've already established, because by the time the poor drenched boy entered the palazzo, he was already voiceless and fevered.

Although the marriage lasted only five months, it was long enough for Paquito to take important precautions. Don Mamerto Sosa, ever faithful to the Loria lineage, was as expert in the family's genealogies and blazons as he was in the intricate sources of its wealth. His old heart leapt with joy when the young marquess, back from his honeymoon, came to consult him in secret. Diminutive, faded, fragile and dusty as a moth, with shiny diminutive eyes behind glasses and immaculate, diminutive hands that handled immaculate documents, Don Mamerto, feeling very proud, rejuvenated by the honor, spent many days locked in his office with Paquito — separated from the rest of his notarial establishment by a door whose upper panel of beveled glass hinted at the silhouettes of office bustle — instructing him in the extent of his possessions and insinuating with great delicacy what measures he considered necessary to neutralize that vulture of a woman — and all of this could only be inferred from allusions couched in the Castillian notary's sober language — who was no more than an upstart Andalusian, when it came down to it, whose behavior was a stain on the family's honor. So far, there had been no financial catastrophe, in spite of her greater tendency toward liquidation than conservation or reinvestment, along with, it couldn't be denied — Don Mamerto declared between throat clearings that seemed to put his very life in danger — something more than carelessness, and which he would even go so far as to call profligacy. From the inquiries the sinful pair had made after Paquito came of age, the notary could infer certain difficulties on the horizon that he didn't like one bit. It was best to remain alert. And since he, Paquito, possessed everything a man could need in terms of suits, cars, trips, and diversions, and his wife had an open account in the most sought-after fashion houses of Madrid, which Don Mamerto's underlings took care of paying, it was recommendable not to do anything, but to take precautions in the case of any possible, though for the moment — praise be to the Holy Virgin — unlikely tragedies: for that, it was enough to sign a will that left everything indisputably in Blanca's hands. Considering that the house's wealth was bounteous enough to cover even trivialities like Tere Castillo's season tickets to the Royal Theater, the best thing would be to go on enjoying the current status quo, and, until the danger showed its face, not to change a thing, or call anything by its true name. Paquito immediately issued the secret will vengefully suggested by Don Mamerto — who, though he seemed otherwise, was a man of strong passions — and instructed Blanca as well in her rights, which for the moment had the elegant quality of being unnecessary to exercise.

In her widowhood, Blanca preferred to seem ignorant of everything and incapable of understanding a thing, like an exquisite luxury doll that wouldn't allow its pretty little head to be filled with tiresome things. However, she enjoyed knowing that both her mother-in-law and Almanza were her dependents — she could freeze all their accounts with a single signature — not to say her servants. Those two, though, were plotting something, because at mourning luncheons they never ceased to suggest how convenient it would be for her to make the most of her time of grief to set off on a voyage to the Americas and visit her family, to arrive there loaded down with gifts. The young widow, grateful as she was for their sage advice, alleged that she didn't yet have the heart to stray far from the fetishes of her adored Paquito. For now, she would content herself with the distraction of her sentimental strolls through Retiro Park.

"Shouldn't you go with her?" Almanza asked Casilda.

"Are you mad?" screeched the marquise, visibly upset by whatever was underlying the count's innocent suggestion. "I detest nature. Don't you know that I can only breathe freely on asphalt, and that I can't tell a willow from a violet?"

And so, every day, if time allowed, and alone, the young dowager marquise of Loria strolled the paths of Retiro decked out in all the mystery of her mourning for the eyes of strangers — for only very occasionally did she see the doffed *canotier* of some friend keeping a respectful distance from her affliction, or else one of Casilda's obsequious relatives approaching. But from her ears hung two tears of wrought gold whose sparkle transcended the veils of grief with perverse winks — the product of the young woman's light step.

These winks from behind the veil were the first thing to elicit a compliment from Tere Castillo when she unexpectedly ran into Blanca, one of them taking a turn around the admirable monument to Don Alfonso XII in one direction, the other going the opposite way:

"Just maddeningly chic!" cried Madame Castillo, shaking hat feathers that were a little out of fashion but still "very her," and which only increased the monumental aspect of a silhouette that was already magnificent in and of itself. "Now, why are you always so alone?"

"How do you know I'm always . . . ?"

"Oh!" replied Tere, malicious but quite incapable of subtlety. "I have a legion of spies who keep me informed of all your doings!"

"Mourning . . . sorrow . . ."

"Rubbish, woman! With how dull that Paquito was! My dear, your husband has left you so well off that you can impose the rules of your mourning as you like, and become Lehár's very heroine here in Madrid! But, who's this coming our way . . . ? Oh, my beloved friend . . ."

The newcomer leaned down to kiss Tere Castillo's outstretched hand, while Blanca meditated on how much she and Paquito had enjoyed hearing Esperanza Iris in the role Tere had mentioned. When this beloved friend straightened up, he tried to calm the unruly puppy he was leading on a chain and at the same time respond to the introductions Tere was making to the marquise of Loria. Blanca examined him. That is, she never came to examine him: the force of that presence pounced on her, confusing her, suffocating her, overtaking her attention so aggressively that she didn't even hear his name or references, the recitation of which for once seemed free of Tere's habitual malevolence.

When the newcomer managed to quiet his puppy, Blanca, as though taking inventory after a fire, calmed down enough to look at him: his muscles, employed in dominating the dog's friskiness, rippled under the black velveteen of his forearms and thighs, while in the shade of the slouch hat—identical to those worn by certain artists she saw in illustrations by Rafael de Penago or by Echea for *La Esfera*—his insolent gaze shone like hardened, freshly cut tar, but also like velvet, and his laugh revealed a powerful tongue and large, wet, carnivorous teeth, surrounded by the exuberance of his coal-black beard. Paquito had been hairless. When Blanca attempted to make small talk like any civilized lady, she found herself incapable of uttering a single word, overwhelmed as she was by the image of that beard sunk between her thighs, the vigor of that tongue delving into her cleft to the point of delirium, those teeth cruelly biting the drenched down of her pubis, the heat of his panting as he dominated the playful puppy straining at the chain; she felt all of her feminine being concentrated in the succulent channel that led to the very depths of her identity.

" . . . my portrait, which Archibaldo is painting, shows me with a kerchief on my head holding a basket of sea bream, as if I were a Galician fisherwoman — me, an Andalusian . . . !" were some snippets of Tere's chatter that Blanca could hardly take in because, her heart shrunk in terror, she felt her tender crevice growing wet from the fever brought on by the painter's presence. So wet that surely he had already perceived her fiery creole aroma, which not even L'Heure Bleue could disguise. The worst part was the damp stain that had doubtless spread on her skirt as the spring breeze blew it against her body. There beside the pond, instead of looking out at the little boats, Archibaldo was examining her from her calves to her waist and chest with shameless glee and no respect for her rank or her grief, as if some pact of youthful sexual exuberance, which excluded Tere, had rendered discretion unnecessary.

But *she* did not have any pact with anyone! She was who she was, the marquise of Loria, lady and mistress of herself and many other people and things! She did not consent to any of it. She couldn't bear the way she blushed, all too aware that her tenacious fantasy about that beard tickling between her legs was making her skirt wet in such a way and in such an obvious place that the painter and that perverse Tere must have noticed, in spite of her attempts to hide it by maneuvering her monkey fur muff. She gave the excuse that she was late for an important appointment with Don Mamerto Sosa — it was the only respectable thing she could think of in that discombobulated moment — and, after summarily taking leave of the pair, who no doubt were lovers, she turned her back on them. She went full speed up the steps from the pond toward the monument, one hand securing her hat which threatened to fly off at any moment, her other hand clasping the muff and holding down her skirt to keep the spring wind from lifting it any higher than the stretch of bare skin where the backs of her knees, between the hem of her dress and the garters clasping her black stockings, were hit by the last burning sparks from the painter's eyes: from below, he was delighting in the spectacle of her flight without even bothering to shush his dog, who barked and barked.

But she wasn't fleeing anything or anyone! she told herself once she was at the top, when she could no longer hear the barking dog and was headed off toward the Puerta de Alcalá. It was true that she had an appointment with Don Mamerto, whose office was two streets down. She quickened her steps along Serrano, as if in that office where everyone obeyed her orders she would find the solace she so sorely needed. Don Mamerto was loyal: he would know how to offer it to her.

She saw her fleeting reflection in the shop windows as she passed: now that the wind had resolutely lifted her widow's veils, the golden tears winked eloquently on her earlobes, and there wasn't a single bootblack or idler who missed the chance to celebrate her with a whistle or lewd comment that was so funny she struggled not to break her austere widow's composure by laughing. Enclosed in the elevator that carried her to the third floor, she felt as though that small, mechanized confessional was like an echo chamber for her frenzied heart, a sealed package for her almost intolerable scent of indignant female mixed with Parisian Guerlain. She flung open the elevator door, flung open the notary office door, and, without a word to the secretaries, whom she had always been careful to treat warmly as a demonstration of the integrity appropriate to her status, she flung open the door to the little room full of yellowed stacks of paper that formed cushions on the floor, on the Chesterfield sofa, and atop the desk, behind which Don Mamerto was barely visible among so many files. The old man had no discernible reaction except to grow pale at the marquise's sudden entrance. She looked so agitated that, without even greeting him with her habitual deference, she sat right down on the corner of his desk, her back to him, and let her head fall defeated over her beautiful chest. A courteous Castilian gentleman in spite of his years, Don Mamerto raised his head after refastening his spats, which he'd undone in order to work more comfortably, and started to get up, clearing his throat and limping. Leaning one hand on his desk, he went over to give the welcome appropriate to his most eminent guest.

As he approached he saw her put one hand over her eyes as if she were about to start sobbing, leaning the weight of her body on her other hand perched on the desk, whose corner, the old man observed, delved deep into the superb elastic flesh of her rump.

His first impulse was to call in the underlings at work on the other side of the beveled glass, ask them to bring salts, or lemon balm tea, or a glass of something stronger. But he didn't, because, as he fitted his diminutive gold-rimmed glasses on his nose to scrutinize this pitiful portrait of suffering, he realized that the marquise's malady was not the kind to be cured with mere potions. Instead, Don Mamerto moved his spotted hand, its skin as wrinkled as a palmiped's, to offer the perhaps more effective consolation of caressing the young woman's own hand as it rested upon the desk.

Blanca saw everything from behind her gloved fingers: the coming and going of the shapes that dissolved in the beveled glass, the old man's endearingly feeble steps as he came closer with a clear desire to please her. And she felt a curious and not disagreeable tightening of her sex at the attractive sight of the tips of immaculately white straps peeking out below his pants and above his spats, surely there to attach his long undergarments to his ankles. As though allowing a grandfather's caress, she permitted Don Mamerto the tender familiarity of his attempt to alleviate her nameless malady with a simple pat on her gloved hand.

"Don't cry, my child . . ." the elderly man was murmuring, now not only sweetly patting her hand but also caressing her marvelous wrist adorned with a very simple Patek Phillippe. "You have everything you need to be happy: youth, beauty, an immense fortune defended by my loyalty, by my entire family and my employees. What more do you want? Of course, poor Paquito . . ."

Blanca shook with a sob upon hearing that beloved name. She almost fainted, and the poor old man found himself with no choice but to support her young body against his own feeble and aged one, circling her waist with a chivalrous arm so the marquise would not collapse. She let her head fall onto that paternal shoulder he offered so generously. Yes, she was soothed by Don Mamerto's mothball smell of decrepitude, like aged starch or yellowed paper. With her gloved hand, Blanca began to slowly caress the old man's leathery face, hairless not from youth but from age, feeling beside her chest the agitated heart of that person whose function was to do anything she wanted: her hand moved over the worried sockets of the notary's eyes, his hollow cheeks, the skin that drooped from his jaw and from the neck that disappeared into the collar of his stiff shirt, descending over his chest toward the frenzied heart, toward his brief little belly beneath his belt, until she reached the place she wanted — the seat of consolation. Out of the corner of her eye, just in case, she watched the shapes outside that, as they passed, froze for an instant in the glass, and she listened for the typewriter's clatter: everything proceeded as normal. She could proceed, too, because Don Mamerto's will to please her was ironclad. She unbuttoned his pants, weeping all the while, her head resting against that paternal man. He seemed diminutive, but clearly he was astonishingly effective for his age, his small horn, aggressive and indomitable, just the exact size, no more and no less, that she needed just then. She raised her skirt and separated her thighs without ever ceasing to whimper or keep watch over the door. The old man's pelvic artistry was such that he entered her with an ease matched by her body, which had been lubricated since Retiro: Blanca stifled a moan of pleasure in Don Mamerto's arms as he rocked, rocking her as well until she sobbed only with delight, undulating her hips, breathing in the comforting perfume of submission, of a thing that was decrepit but normal and clean and virile, while Don Mamerto, imposing his skillful movements onto hers, rose to a rapid rhythm in which she let herself be carried away, her thighs raised, skirt around her waist, sitting on the corner of the desk, her hat's veils covering the head of the old man panting beside her. Blanca didn't feel Don Mamerto's hands. Where had that wonderful man — who didn't need them to excite her or to excite himself — put them? In the whirlwind of those minutes of dangerous madness, Don Mamerto's breathing faltered dangerously, as did hers, growing so intermittent that, at the moment when he flooded her and she responded by squeezing him with a short and violent orgasm, he went perfectly and suddenly still, as if he wanted to prolong all this by taking it with him into eternity, faint and breathless, like her. The old man and the young marquise remained joined for a second in that embrace, while she examined her own mind to determine the appropriate attitude to take upon separating. Don Mamerto was, in truth, very small, very light, so fragile that she could have lifted him like a bird, so delicate that she might crush him if she gripped him between her legs when she lowered her thighs to pull her skirt back down over her garters and the twisted stockings that had fallen below her knees. While Blanca decided on a protocol to follow after undoing the embrace, which had to happen now, he remained inside her, though of course completely lifeless now. Terrified at this thought, and realizing that Don Mamerto was sliding down her own very alive body, falling slowly and as empty and shapeless as a lightweight nightshirt, incapable of holding on to anything, Blanca started to stand up. Detached from her, Don Mamerto fell to the floor soundlessly, bone-white and inert.

The marquise brought a hand to her mouth to stifle the rising scream of terror, but managed to think and to stop it in time. Immediately, she got down on her knees beside the body, put the old man's benevolent member into his underwear, buttoned his fly and wiped away the stains that love had left on his pants. She took a diamond and tortoiseshell comb from her purse and used it to smooth her friend's few tousled hairs, and she arranged his body on the floor so it looked like he'd fallen naturally. Beside him, she placed a file she found on the desk that concerned the sale of ten thousand walnut trees on a country property of the Lorias' in Andalusia. Then she hurriedly arranged her own attire, refreshed her eyeliner, blush, and powder, pulled up her stockings and attached them to the garters, and straightened her hat with a long pin. Then, looking at Don Mamerto Sosa dead at her feet, she was pierced by the pain of the old man's death in such an intimate situation, and terrified by a loss that left her defenseless against those hyenas, her mother-in-law and the count of Almanza. Blanca Loria let out a shriek, which was immediately attended to by the notary employees and Don Mamerto's sons. Only then did Blanca allow herself to faint.

4

THE YOUNG DOWAGER MARQUISE OF LORIA WAS NOT, HOW-
ever, without her defenses.

At the funeral held at Los Jerónimos Church (attended by all the
women—Blanca, Casilda, Tere Castillo, all dressed in such strict black
it was as though they were mourning a member of their own family),
as she went down the receiving line of the bereaved, the young marquise was able to verify something that she had never realized before
and that brought her great peace of mind: Don Mamerto was not a
unique or irreplaceable specimen. On the contrary, what seemed to
be a series of carbon copies of the deceased stood in a line from oldest
to youngest, and they shook hands and climbed into the procession
cars like a line of those toy ducks with heads that bob in unison when
they move: Don Mamerto's sons and grandsons, all diminutive, all
yellowish, and all, no doubt, unconditionally faithful to Blanca, now
the possessor of the House of Loria's wealth. The youngest Mamerto's
wife was carrying a diapered baby in her arms. After the procession
was out of sight, when the disconsolate wives stood for a while on
the steps outside the church to comment on the magnificence of the
flowers the young marquise had ordered the place filled with—all
white, like a wedding, they observed—Blanca asked the deceased's
daughter-in-law to let her hold his grandson . . . although perhaps he
was a great-grandson. While she rocked him in her arms and caressed
him tenderly, she delved into his diaper to see if the child, whose
features were so similar to Don Mamerto's, was also identical down

37

below: as soon as she touched it, the tiny little horn stood at attention, putting itself at her service just like the deceased's had, and, Blanca supposed, as would those of the fortunately innumerable Mamertos. The marquise's verdict, offered to the attendees through the tears of her sobbing that so moved them all, was that, over time, the darling child she held in her arms would be the spitting image, both spiritually and physically, of the exemplary man that had been the notary Don Mamerto Sosa.

"These mawkish Americans just can't miss a chance to make a scene," she heard Casilda comment to Tere Castillo sotto voce.

Blanca overheard Tere's reply as well, insinuating that it was all part of "that foreigner's" strategy to get the Sosa family on her side; she, however, had no doubt that even without her tears — which, moreover, were entirely genuine — any problems she brought to the dead man's family would be met with countless members willing to attend her with the same exquisite deference as Don Mamerto had on that fateful occasion.

The afternoon of the day following the burial, largely to reassure herself of this fidelity, Blanca put in an appearance at the Sosa family's office. As her thoughts were occupied by other matters, she didn't come with a specific problem to present them with; instead, she proposed the first thing that came into her head when she saw the new Mamerto rise to receive her from behind the same folder-strewn desk that his father had once occupied and invite her to take a seat at the other end of the Chesterfield sofa. To wit: she told him that she wished to commission a full-length portrait of Paquito dressed up in his Icarus costume, to hang alongside his forebears in Alarcón de los Arcos. She asked the notary to contact, on her behalf, Archibaldo Arenas, currently a very sought-after portraitist among those in the know. Could he be so kind as to consult on prices, send the painter photographs of Paquito along with what was left of the disguise and wings, request a sketch, and set a delivery deadline? The notary, after taking note of the matter, begged the marquise to accompany him to an interview with the other Sosas of the firm, all descendants of the deceased Don Mamerto; upon learning of Madame Marquise's visit, they had all gathered and were waiting for her.

There must have been eight or ten of these Sosas who, after swarming about Blanca to kiss her hand, arranged themselves around a large table and beseeched her to sit at its head. They were of a mind to inform her about certain small but confidential matters that, according to the Mamerto who had received her today—or maybe a different one, for when the old were mixed in with the equally diminutive young ones, it was not only very difficult to distinguish him, but also impossible to comprehend what they were explaining—urgently needed to be resolved. Instead of taking an interest in the serious matters they were trying to expound upon, her pretty little head, wrapped in an oilcloth cloche with a silver buckle over one ear, turned to look at the Sosas one by one, old, young, very young, placing them in a line on the table and disrobing them there by order of height so as to check how effectively she could stimulate each one with the naked sarabande she was dancing for them, and how quickly they fell dead one by one at the touch of her body: those starched collars, those neat little hands on the tabletop as though about to pray, those eyes behind glasses gazing incredulously at her inattentive frivolity, at the smile that rose to her lovely pursed lips, at the laugher that bloomed at the sight of a family so composed while so completely nude, at the burst of hilarity that Blanca could not hold back in the end. They gave her a glass of water to calm her poor nerves, as the most cultured of the Sosas noted, "Ridi pagliaccio . . . " so the others would respect the depths of the sensitive marquise's suffering.

Once she was calmer, the lead Mamerto tried to explain with the utmost discretion that in the absence of the elder dowager marquise, Madame Casilda, who had just left for Paris to buy her summer wardrobe for the beaches of Biarritz, the count of Almanza, perhaps out of an excess of familiarity, perhaps by mistake, had appropriated the substantial funds recently brought in from the sale of the yield of an Andalusian walnut farm (which had been the property of the Lorias — that is, *my* property, Blanca told herself—since time immemorial)

39

to a Swiss chocolate factory, and used the money to buy an English racehorse of impeccable pedigree but still unpredictable performance.

"Almanza?" asked Blanca, suddenly alert as a bloodhound picking up the scent of its prey.

As she asked them to repeat everything in detail, complete with figures and transaction dates, so she could listen carefully this time, she could not help but disrobe that absent gentleman, who, placed upon the counsel's table, won out over the diminutive Sosas not only in size but also in all the muscled virility of his sportive forty years: evoking him was like letting a breath of fresh air into that stuffy office, like an elegant animal presence amid so much paper, the very incarnation of wantonness, aplomb, and pleasure in the midst of so much integrity and obligation. Yes. Almanza was a rogue. Paquito had already warned her of that. But careful not to overstep: she, at the end of the day, was an untamed female from the new continent, a fact she was not ashamed of even if she chose to varnish it with a coat of civilization — a coat she was ready to destroy as soon as it was meet to do so, especially if it meant taking revenge on a cynic who was trying to make her his next victim. Not a word to Almanza, she told the astonished Sosas. She would take care of settling accounts with him. For the time being they were not to pay any of the bills Casilda sent from Paris, or give her any explanation. Blanca was fed up. So fed up that if they continued to vex her she was ready to liquidate all her holdings and buy half of Nicaragua to exploit it as she pleased, leaving Casilda and Almanza in the lurch. Seeing the consternation written on the Sosas' faces at this proposal, which would make them paupers as well, she decided to leave all those ideas floating inconclusively in the air. She departed, repeating that she was fed up with all the humiliation, and barely saying goodbye to the Sosas, who were all standing openmouthed around the table.

Blanca walked two blocks down Serrano without stopping in front of a single shop window. At the Puerta de Alcalá she looked down at her Patek Philippe: yes, though it was a little late, she still had at least another hour under the lovely sky of that Madrid evening, and she could spend it on a walk through Retiro to forget the recent unpleasantness.

But it cannot be said that on this occasion Blanca Loria delighted in the dusk nor in the park itself exactly, for at the very moment she entered, as if he had been waiting for her, Archibaldo Arenas loomed up—in his cape and big black slouch hat, with his gray dog pulling its leash taut and seeming about to escape—and his figure entirely blocked the landscape, occupying the marquise's whole visual field. But he greeted her so unaffectedly that after the first moment of consternation, Blanca felt perfectly at ease strolling the paths and avenues with such a genteel companion. They both laughed as they talked about Tere Castillo and the difficulties she presented as a model, how one day she wanted to be painted as a denizen of Madrid in the style of Anglada Camarasa, and then, once the canvas was well underway, she'd take a fancy to posing thoughtfully with her elbow on a Greek column, and then again as an English horse rider . . . who knows how long she would remain satisfied with her basket of sea bream à la Álvarez de Sotomayor . . . Tere was impossible, they both declared, but they also agreed she was a very amusing character, which quite made up for it.

They fell silent for a moment, standing next to each other, the dog quiet beside them as if he understood, gazing out at the lemon-gray water of the lake, so pleasant as the sun set. The painter removed his hat to let the air blow freely through his magnificent black mane: the light bathing his face revealed a youth Blanca had not previously noticed in his features, which were nearly as vulnerable—though her mute plea was: no, dear God, not quite so vulnerable this time—as Paquito's. And she didn't know whether it was a pleasant or unpleasant surprise that she felt when she noticed that the painter's eyes were not absolutely black, as she had believed, but rather transparent, gray or lemon-colored like the water they were contemplating, and—she realized with a shiver that reintegrated her sensitive spirit with the magnificent instrument of the senses that was her body—exactly the same color as the dog's eyes. The dog, like them, was gazing at the water of the lake: moon-colored eyes, Blanca thought. And because she'd lose her mind if she allowed all of this to envelop her, she asked Archibaldo:

"What's his name?"

"Whose?"

"The dog's."

"Luna."

"But it's not a female . . ."

Blanca blushed at her own words, for they gave away the fact that she had observed something quite inappropriate for a lady: that the most caressable light-gray flannel, which swathed Luna's whole body, also covered that part of his anatomy which was ugly to look at and which had led her to utter her ill-considered sentence. Blanca turned serious, stiff, very chic, with her eyes staring off into space so that her abstraction would keep her from feeling — as she had been feeling since her own words had reignited in her a series of pressing needs that, for the moment, she rejected — this urge to run away and disappear somewhere where neither the man nor the dog could ever find her. And yet neither could she stifle the opposite urge, equally strong, to lean her body over slightly to feel a little, just a little, of the warm nearness of Archibaldo's body. Luna, as though he understood, came to her rescue, madly frisking about once again, possessed by a frenetic compulsion that Blanca would prefer not to decipher so as not to have to decipher it in herself. Archibaldo, meanwhile, used language that blended authority and tenderness as well as the nervous strength of his arms to try and calm the puppy, which wrapped Blanca up in its leash as it gamboled. Untangling her, Archiboldo made an imperious gesture to dominate the dog, and in doing so knocked Blanca's cloche to the ground; her tresses spilled over her shoulders.

"Why don't you let that poor animal off the leash?" she asked, once she was untangled and had returned the cloche to her head and they began to walk again, too quickly because Luna was tugging at the leash.

"Don't wear the hat . . ."

"Are you crazy? Go without a hat in public? You don't like it?"

"Just as you were a moment ago, with the lemon-gray lake as a background and your hair loose — I would like to paint your portrait like that."

"Impossible, because I'm going to cut it *à la garçonne*, which is all the rage."

"I forbid you from doing such a mad thing."

"But why don't you let that poor animal loose? That way we could stroll more peacefully . . ."

"He is very young and stupid, he could get lost."

"Poor thing."

The sun was setting. No one was walking through Retiro at that hour. Unwittingly — or had Archibaldo, who had surely done this with other women, manipulated the situation? — they suddenly found themselves in a place nearly closed off by somber hedges. With a terrified shudder of her sex, Blanca thought that here, without anyone being the wiser, he or anyone else could strangle her — with Luna's leash, for example. But Luna was barking and jumping because he wanted to play, and almost as if he'd been trained to do it, he again encircled Blanca with his leash. While the painter's hands freed her, she was deciding that the moment had come to grow cross with him. Before she could follow through on that plan, however, he took her in his arms. She could not help but struggle a little so as to press her delicious body, which she seemed to know fully for the first time ever, closer against Archibaldo's, who was trying to separate her thighs with a desperate knee. Even as she pretended to resist, she surrendered little by little, more and more, and even as she refused him her lips she allowed him to kiss her entire face, her neck, her collarbone, until she couldn't stand it anymore and gave him her mouth, which he opened with his own, snatching her breath away as his eager tongue delved into her: he had to let go of the dog, which dashed off to disappear among the shadows of the park, dragging its leash behind it. Archibaldo slid his hand under her skirt, and Blanca did not miss that hand's delighted surprise when it found that since she was not wearing underwear it could touch the satiny skin of her hips, the sweet curve of her belly that led downward to the wet softness of the forest that the hand began to caress. She took her mouth from his to murmur into his ear:

"Not here . . ."

"Where?"

"Don't you want to paint my portrait?"

"In my studio, then."

They were still kissing, touching each other.

"How many others, there . . . ?"

"What does it matter?"

It doesn't, thought Blanca. And then Luna was back, so playful and happy he leapt up as though to kiss Archibaldo, to kiss Blanca, until they had no choice but to separate. While he picked up his dog's leash, she straightened her clothing and heard him pleading with her: "When, when . . . ?"

They emerged from the grove and walked toward the road.

"Tomorrow . . . at six. Let's meet as though by chance at the Royal House of the Post Office, at the front door . . ."

But it was around Blanca, not Archibaldo, that Luna pranced and danced, celebrating her, leaping heavily onto her, making her laugh. In the dog's rare moments of calm, Blanca petted him while the three of them headed toward the Puerta de Alcalá exit, because night was starting to fall.

"You go out this way," Blanca said, "through the Lagasca gate . . . I'll go out through the other one. Until tomorrow . . ."

"Goodbye . . ."

As Blanca walked away, Luna started to whine and leap about so much that she had to stop and turn back, laughing.

"What's wrong, Luna, dear?"

"He wants to go with you."

"Poor thing . . . !"

"Why do you pity him?"

"Those who grow attached to me tend to suffer."

Paquito. Don Mamerto. But, laughing, the painter challenged her: "Not this one."

44

"Could be the exception."

"Could be . . ."

"In any case, if one escapes suffering, the other will not."

That was the sort of thing the black women had told her, things she read in Zamacois or Alberto Insúa. Archibaldo hesitated a moment, then impulsively, offered her the leash: "To prove my trust, let me give him to you as a gift."

"Are you mad . . . ?"

Offended, she felt as though this proposal held out an ersatz version of intimacy with him—not a medicine, but a placebo. Or was he suggesting, rather, an intimacy much riskier than that which they had shared thus far, even greater than what she was proposing they share tomorrow as of six p.m.? Confused, she turned her back on the man and on the dog who wanted to follow her, turning her little steps toward the Puerta de Alcalá.

It was—thought Blanca as she hurried to the exit—as if many things were boiling inside her: desire, shame, fear, rage. The desire she accepted and enjoyed, even as searingly obsessive as it was. And the shame and fear, well, when it came down to it, a lady like her . . . and in a public place where she would never dare show her face without a hat in the latest style. But why the rage? Why this tremendous rage that made her eyes tear up, ruining the eyeliner that she had reapplied as she left Retiro? No, it wasn't rage against Archibaldo, all sensitive tendon and nerve, all sweet determination to share a unique intimacy with her, who was utterly unfamiliar with it. This was a different rage. Rage at feeling humiliated, used, abused, as if avid teeth were tearing at the lovely flesh that made her so proud: Almanza. Yes. Almanza. When she located her rage precisely, the count's name leapt automatically into her consciousness. Yes, Almanza. Don Mamerto—oh, well, a Mamerto who was not, of course, the real Don Mamerto—had said it that very afternoon. In front of the Puerta de Alcalá, with night already fallen, she paused for a moment: she would return to the Mamertos' office to get more information she could use to humiliate the count. She looked at her Patek Phillippe. No, it was too late. All the

45

Mamertos, each with the woman and children that corresponded to his age, were resting from a day of honest work around their brazier tables. Without thinking—she realized only once she was even with Calle Juan de Mena—she had been hurrying down Alfonso XII. She crossed to the other sidewalk and went as far as Ruiz de Alarcón. Yes, because on top of everything, the beautiful apartment building on Ruiz de Alarcón where the count of Almanza lived without paying a dime of rent belonged to Paquito—that is, to her. She had the idea to go and immediately express to the count—since she happened to be in the vicinity of his house—that he may very well be a count, but to her he was no more than a crook of the very worst sort.

When the marquise of Loria entered and said to the porter, "the count of Almanza?" he, either because she looked so beautiful and walked with such confidence, or else because Almanza, in spite of his long-standing entanglement with Casilda, received frequent visits from women who came to give themselves to him, didn't put up the slightest obstacle. Taking the elevator up, Blanca sat on a small red velvet bench to give a final touch-up to her lips—now with good lighting—which Archibaldo's amorous excesses had smeared. No, she told herself: displaying her rage would be unbecoming for a worldly woman who could afford the luxury of remaining above such trifles. On the contrary, if Almanza and Casilda planned to use her, as they clearly did, she would use Almanza, who at the end of the day was just one more of her many servants. She had to admit that, though she had confidence in her own instincts for such things, she would rather Archibaldo not notice her inexperience tomorrow, since neither Paquito nor Don Mamerto counted as real experience. Almanza, a renowned layabout, could at least repay her generosity by training her for the next day's tryst, for it was said that he was an expert in matters of love.

Aside from that, she had to admit as well that she was a little afraid of hurting Archibaldo, because her enamored body—flesh that is too beautiful, like hers, was a matter of witchcraft, the dark old women of her childhood whispered during the nights when she was a little girl who couldn't sleep because the moon wasn't out—could hurt the very person who was destined to make her happy. But that was the nonsense of primitive people: she was the marquise of Loria, she wore a very simple but quite fashionable dress by Drecoll, she read Rubén Darío and Villaespesa in her leisure time, she had attended the odd lecture by García Sanchiz, she drank tea at the Ritz, and no harm, as such, could befall her. She opened her compact, which was embossed with the image of a swan, and dabbed a puff of perfumed powder on the tip of her nose. Then she rang the bell.

Almanza, dressed in purple satin Cossack's pajamas but wearing some sort of horrible mask to flatten his mustache, opened the door a crack, then slammed it closed. After a moment, now with his mustache freed and waxed, opened his front door wide for Blanca.

"Can I come in . . . ?" she asked timidly, stammering in the threshold.

"What an honor!"

Almanza explained that he had just now finished doing his exercises, which was why she found him like that, en déshabillée. That is, he had been amusing himself—and now that Casilda was out of town he did have a lot of free time on his hands—by lifting weights: she could see them for herself in the corner, beside his modest library.

"Oh! You are an intellectual!" she exclaimed, walking over to the shelves, not without first noting that her mother-in-law's hand held despotic dominion over that apartment's decoration, leaving only an insignificant corner for the count's few trophies. Moreover, Blanca observed, it was a relatively small apartment, which showed Casilda's greedy propensity to pinch every penny she could so as to lavish more pleasures upon herself.

"Caballero Audaz . . . Felipe Trigo . . . Vargas Vila . . . Hernández Catá . . ." Blanca was reading the books' spines, her back turned to Almanza, who followed her a little confusedly because he couldn't fathom the reason for such an untimely visit. She turned around sharply to face him, and asked: "Do you read Rubén Darío?"

Their two faces, now, were very close; Almanza's was frozen in a smile of incredulous joy.

"Did you know he is a compatriot of mine?"

The count took only a few seconds to absorb the possible meaning of the fact that, upon uttering the divine Rubén's name, she brought her youthful face two centimeters closer — no more, but two centimeters full of delicious intention — to his. He stuttered a little as he replied: "But ... but of course." Recovering instantly, though, he went on in a more appropriate style: "What man who claims to have a sensitive soul — in sum, to be civilized — is ignorant of the lines 'The air was gentle, circling slowly...?' But Blanca, why are we still standing? Come over here, please, sit down, make yourself comfortable on the divan, here, I'll place this cushion behind your back so you'll be more at ease, and this other one here for you to rest your arm. A little higher, perhaps? No? Well then, if you're more comfortable like that ... What a lovely dress! I salute you, you're one of the few women in Madrid who know how to reconcile chic with mourning. Would you like something to drink ... a little Pernod ...? Some tea? What a shame that it's precisely my waitstaff's day off."

Or does Casilda, when she's away, cut off your allowance and leave you without servants in order to save money? Not because she really wanted anything, but just to make him work while she slowly removed her gloves, as though peeling a delectable fruit, Blanca stammered:

"Let's see ... I don't know ... perhaps ..."

Almanza was certainly *un bel homme*, with his pectoral muscles — a bit too much for Blanca, who dreamed of feline lovers — accentuated under the violet satin of his Cossack's blouse. And his utterly empty but stately head — and she should know, for her continent produced abundant harvests of such men! — placed like a statue's atop the classical frame of his neck and shoulders. As Almanza looked at her, ready to obey her wishes — which, as was fitting, were his commands — Blanca noticed that the count breathed in such a way that his chest puffed up and the nostrils of his aquiline nose flared, while his left eyebrow arched simultaneously, almost imperceptibly.

"Although I don't ... but yes. Yes. A cup of tea ...?" she asked.

And she dropped her gloves beside her low-heeled patent shoe. Instantly, Almanza knelt down beside her to pick them up. Blanca took that moment to cross one leg over the other so that the silk of her skirt would slide up to reveal her knee, and, just above the garter, exactly where the count's mustache was, a centimeter of taut skin adorned with a tiny mole. Kneeling, he tried to intertwine his passionate gaze with hers. Blanca avoided his eyes. Still, Almanza planted a light kiss on that little mole, tickling it pleasantly with his mustache, and he was about to continue the caress up her thigh, Blanca thought as she blushed in enchanted embarrassment. But no: only if she allowed it. And she was not willing to allow him that frivolous style, which clearly came so easily to him. Instead, she dealt him a blow to his left eye. She leapt to her feet, enraged at the magnitude of his affront. He stood up as well, also enraged, the eye under the recently arched brow now tearing up, his chest almost touching Blanca's nipples, standing at attention under her silk dress. They both panted with rage, their breath commingling, the passion in their eyes entwined. Blanca calculated that she had less than half a second to decide: kiss or don't kiss those mustache-shaded lips. Instead, she struck Almanza again, with her other hand this time, in his other eye, and cried: "Scoundrel!"

And another slap: "Heel! I shall tell my mother-in-law!"

This time Almanza managed to catch her hand. With one shove he toppled her onto the divan's cushions and fell upon that buxom body struggling against his own. He slid his practiced hands underneath her skirt, immediately finding there the electrical center that turned on and grew wet, at which point Almanza did not doubt his victory. Blanca, ablaze, kicked in spite of it all, and scratched, while he was tearing at her dress to expose her breasts and bite them mercilessly, making her squeal with indignation between the insults her pretty mouth was hurling at him — thief, rascal, old codger, shameless crook, the walnut farm, the horse, Casilda, the apartment, cynic, hypocrite — as she crossed her thighs to reject those caresses, which were not caresses but rather an insulting aggression of refined technique, and to keep the count from reaching the inner secret of her body with that iron crowbar whose force was separating their two bodies, now almost naked amidst the tatters of their clothing. If Almanza wanted it, let

49

him take the trouble to rape her, even as her sharply filed fingernails scratched the count's face until he bled and tore his Cossack's blouse to expose his woolly pectorals. His own insults — whore, mawkish tattletale, did she think he couldn't tell, enough with the pretense, when he could smell her desire a mile away, what had she come to his house for, after all, slut — only made her fiercer, and she refused to give her mouth to him or relax her thighs while the two of them writhed together atop the cushions. Who did this damned American think she was . . . ! Almanza flattened her with his powerful body. He took a satin cushion and pressed it against that face made more beautiful by the terror and rage and clear desire: yes, let her be afraid. Let her suffocate from terror in front of him, a real man, not a wimp like Paquito. Let her try to insult him now, when she couldn't even breathe.

When the fear — for it could be nothing else — finally made her lay inert and relax her marvelous thighs, the count entered her with one of his famous thrusts, and felt the splendid gluttony with which she devoured him. He removed the cushion he had pressed against her face, gloriously beautiful with her weeping eyes closed, but he wanted to see them open, shining, round and lively, the way he liked: he withdrew his member from the cocoon that enveloped it. Only then, displeased, did Blanca open her eyes imploringly, terrified of losing all, and, encircling the count's waist with the knot of her thighs, she pulled him back down on top of her. She opened her lips to accept his mouth and devour his tongue.

This time, then, he penetrated her gently, as he knew so well how to do — even making it seem unintentional — reaching depths of her person that the dowager marquise of Loria hadn't even suspected she possessed, as time stretched out, dusky, hot and wet, into what seemed to both of them a perfectly satisfying version of the infinite.

5

SO THEN THIS WAS . . . ?

The hour grew late and she could not sleep. Tossing between her bedsheets under the new baldachin, she was kept awake as though by the howls of a pack of beasts that were entirely unrelated, to be sure, with the count of Almanza, who was many things, but no beast. He had implored her with his most saccharine words to stay and spend the night with him. But Blanca refused, warning him that not now and not ever would she be willing to violate convention, since to her, definitive luxury consisted in obeying it: her staff, for one thing, would be very surprised if she arrived home even a little late, especially when they had seen her go out after lunch in such simple attire, headed for the notary's office. She didn't need to remind a gentleman like him that one needed to take care even with such small details when living in this big village that subsisted on gossip, as if it were inhabited solely by porters and concierges. Contradicting himself in his attempt to convince her—Blanca would never forget that in a fit of rage he'd called her mawkish, an accusation an American cannot forget—Almanza exhorted her to be bold, assuring her that her position in Madrid was so secure that she could do whatever she liked and people would always respect her, because the Loria fortune—that is, *her* fortune—was . . . well, just that, respectable.

It must have been eleven at night when the dozing porter opened up for Blanca, who rushed past him inside so he wouldn't notice the

tatters of her lovely dress. But she could not sleep. Was it twelve o'clock
. . . ? twelve thirty . . . ? Perhaps she should take Veronal, like Casilda?
She had been tossing and turning between the sheets for an eternity.
In spite of the abrasive howling in the street, she felt as though the
count of Almanza's skillful caresses had tuned her body like an exqui-
sitely sensitive instrument, transforming it into a sumptuous object
of the softest silk: never had it been so beautiful, nor so full, so young
or so light. Several times during her inexplicable insomnia she had
risen from her nest of strawberry-colored satin to gaze at herself naked in the mirror that hung in that marriage bedroom-cum-widow's
chamber. She entertained herself for a while — in those moments,
the barking seemed like mere distant echoes — practicing before the
mirror, alone, or rather with her own shadow, some of the poses of love
that the count of Almanza, with his inexhaustible knowledge of those
arts, had just taught her, and which she planned to apply tomorrow.
Because, in spite of all the pleasure, it had been but practice. Same
as with Paquito. Same as with Don Mamerto . . .

Was it the neighbor's dog that was barking and keeping her awake?
It usually sounded indistinct, as if from far away. And yet that night the
sound was multiplied, and too close by. But in the end, now that she had
"lived," she had much to think about, much to remember: the limbo of
her mind was no longer haunted only by the inefficient spirits of her two
previous victims. Fleetingly, she thought that Almanza, after dropping
her off in his modest but brand-new Ford — which she had financed, no
doubt — drunk on love, might very well have crashed into a tree on his
drive back to Ruiz de Alarcón, perishing instantly and hopefully spilling
very little blood, all because of his contact with her. But no: Almanza
would not die tonight, because he had felt no emotion for her, nor she
for him. Pleasure, yes: all the pleasure imaginable, all that she would
never have dared imagine. But feeling him as a person, as a human
being incorporated into that pleasure and enjoying it along with her,
as an attempt to take two distinct, private fantasies and make a single
one, braiding them into an exciting give-and-take of unexchangeable
people — no, not that. Which is why Almanza, who was not vulnerable,

would not die. Lying naked on the divan's cushions afterwards, she had wept a little because of that, but since she preferred not to explain her tears to someone who could not understand them, she'd told him she was crying because she was so alone, without parents or relatives, a foreigner in spite of her title and fortune, and because he did not respect her; in sum, because she had no one who would defend her. Which prompted Almanza to observe, "Frankly, my dear Blanca, I believe that in this battle it is I, not you, who needs defending."

She dried her tears and replied, "Well . . . yes."

And then it was Blanca who raped the count right then and there on the Persian rug beside the divan. Now, with the unsettling racket outside that would not let her sleep, she thought enviously that the count of Almanza, sated, would have downed a good drink of cognac and must now be sprawled out asleep, perhaps even snoring, his mustache covers on.

Blanca turned over in bed again, drawing the sheet over her head. She remembered how when she was very, very little, people were always promising her a trip to the ocean as a reward if she behaved, especially the mestiza women who had never seen the sea themselves and moreover lacked the power to bestow such a prize on her: how immense it was, they said, the horizon so vast, so blue, interminable waves as far as the eye could see. When, at long last and after so much waiting, she was finally taken on that trip and from a hilltop laid eyes on the sea for the very first time, she told her astonished family: "It's not as big as they said it was!"

A thing that existed only in the word of people who knew nothing of it, that was no more than the expression of a legend, a fantasy — that was what Blanca missed in her first sighting of the sea: a thing that was even more than the something it certainly was. The night with Almanza was like the delight of sinking down into the warm swells of the Caribbean, like swimming in the safety of that pure aquamarine, like feeling all the salt and sun of childhood designing the shape of her body, like letting herself go, be rocked, lulled . . . all quite essential, quite wonderful. But she was missing the same thing that she had missed in that first view of the sea when she was so young that she allowed herself to feel truths and speak them aloud: it was, decidedly, not the devastating adventure projected by the magnificent ambiguity of the word, especially the word refracted in the imagination of those who, one way or another, are prevented from experiencing it.

Still, she did plan to use Almanza again. Last night he had proposed that they run away together, even, if she so desired, to Nicaragua, where they could easily have themselves declared the equivalent of king and queen. He admitted he was sick of Casilda, of her coldness and avarice, her insufferable narcissism that demanded everyone bow down before her: the repetition of a sin turned it sacred, and then it was the most boring thing in the world. Blanca allowed herself the pleasure of laughing in his face at the marriage proposal—for that's what it was—objecting that the alliance did not benefit her at all, and neither was it a union of love like with Paquito, though she was careful not to confide the shortcomings that had plagued said union. As she listened to the barking dog keeping her awake, she realized that what had made her reject Almanza was, in essence, the fact that she could not kill him: he was not vulnerable. He left something— wisely, no doubt, and perhaps many things, she suspected—outside of the bed of love; at no point did he offer himself as a victim of her divine and infernal embrace, as had Don Mamerto, for example, whom age had turned so vulnerable that she could knock him over, so to speak, with a feather, or poor Paquito, who had surrendered to her completely within his regrettable limitations. The count of Almanza's impeccable performance had been pure skill, pure technique, pure mechanics—which had all existed before her, and had nothing to do with her. The rhythm, the audacity, the crescendo calculated even in its flat notes, the caresses, the search, the astonishing discovery of the most sensitive places of her anatomy, venturing first here, then there, all that calculated heterodoxy: yes, it was like a master class. But no more than that.

But what more did she want, when that was precisely what she was looking for at Calle Ruiz de Alarcón?

If the neighbor's dog weren't barking so, perhaps she could manage to find an answer that would satisfy her poor nerves, at least for tonight. The sheets were boiling, wrapping her in burning heat not from the ardor of the count's powerful muscles, but rather an accursed fever. The palliative, as always, was to be found in herself: with the light out, the sheet covering her, she caressed her much-loved body until she reached the "sunken pearl of the navel," as the count had called it, eliciting mere laughter with a line of Darío's poetry that moved her deeply when she read it. She probed there, and further down, in the tenderness of fur that was nearly not animal, searching for her obedient center that had never failed her. Without touching it at first, simply rocking her hips and rubbing her thighs together with a force that came from her very vertex, letting the threads of the sheet just barely caress the tips of her nipples, she was sensing something that, even as her imagination was evoking Almanza first, as the most skilled, then Paquito, as the most loved, then poor old Don Mamerto, she would never be able to feel . . . unless she felt it tomorrow with Archibaldo. But, above all, she couldn't treat it as a project: Archibaldo awaited her, ardent, beautiful, lively. He was going to take her beyond mere pleasure and thus make her pleasure complete. Evoking the painter's figure beside the lemon-gray water of the twilight that was reflected in his eyes, Blanca, almost without moving, not touching herself, went right up to the very edge as never before, and was about to dive into the water of those eyes when the unbearable barking rose up like a surging wave right beneath her window, insistent, demented, demanding. Furious, Blanca leapt from the bed and flung open the window. In the dark street below, between the palazzo's bars, she recognized a prancing and whining animal shape that was darker than the night. Two lemon-gray eyes shone as they looked up at her through the bars.

"Luna . . ." she exclaimed very quietly, then ducked behind the shutter.

She peered out at the dog, whose presence was inexplicable.

"Go," she ordered in a soft whisper, knowing the dog would neither hear her nor obey.

But Luna, once he knew—could he smell her?—that she was watching him from behind the window lattice, only redoubled his barking. Now she saw the silhouette of his body standing up, front paws on the gate, barking right at her as though to convince her of something. Blanca feared that in the solitary street a night watchman would come and shoo Luna away, or, worse, catch him. She had to do something. She wasn't going to leave that poor, crazy dog whining outside her house all night long.

She closed the shutter stealthily—the dog must not think she was ignoring him—and opened her closet, took out a pink brocade peignoir and put it over her light nightgown. Turning on few lights, taking care not to wake anyone, not even her maid sleeping a few doors down, she descended to the ground floor and went to the front door, where she unlocked the bolts. Then she walked down the steps, crossed the small front yard, opened the gate and went out to the sidewalk. Or rather, she tried to: she didn't get a chance, because as soon as she opened the gate, Luna, who was waiting quietly for her outside, lunged at her, jumping and kissing her but no longer whining, as if he didn't want to give away his presence beside Blanca in the center of a secret that enveloped them both. She brought the dog inside the gate and closed it. They walked down the gravel path lined with high rosebushes as she talked to the dog, soothing him, petting his back. "We have to go inside nice and quiet," she said, "so no one knows we're together; we can't wake anyone up, because they might think it strange that we know each other." She patted Luna's soft coat of gray flannel and together they went up the front steps and through the door, which she closed behind them, and then up the marble stair guarded only by the eyes, now blind, of the cranes in the stained glass window.

Once they were in her bedroom, Blanca began asking Luna why he had come to seek her out and visit her, why he'd fled his owner's house, why he'd chosen her from among so many. Meanwhile, she turned on all the lights, so that the silver and crystal of her dressing table shone, as did the mirrors, and the bronze of the furniture, and the satin, and the teardrop crystals of the chandelier. Luna sat down: his supremely intelligent eyes admired it all, and then gazed at her as though approving of all that opulence.

"Would you like something to eat?" Blanca asked, as she would with any guest. "Or drink?"

Luna stared at her to accept the offering. Blanca implored him to be a good boy while she went to get him something. What do dogs eat? Meat, she supposed, and she went down to the kitchen in search of some. She found a few bloody pieces that, in spite of her initial disgust, looked appetizing once she piled them on a plate. She washed her fingers and gathered the folds of her pink robe. With the dish of raw meat in hand, she went back up the marble stairs and entered her room, double-locking the door behind her. She looked around for Luna amid all the shining silver and crystal: she found him curled up on one end of the bed in a nest of satin, contemplating her entrance with his astonishing eyes. He didn't jump down from the bed until she called him: "Luna, come . . ."

She set the dish on the rug. The dog, calmly, without lunging, devoured all the meat, licking the blood from the edges of the plate until it was perfectly clean. Then he jumped back up on the bed and curled up, satisfied, in the spot where he'd been before and which he seemed to have appropriated. Blanca removed her robe. After turning out all the lights, she opened the window a little to let in the spring breeze, then climbed into bed.

Now that the dog had eaten well and was settled in that room whose luxury he had approved, he would no longer bark or whine. He would let her sleep. But Blanca still saw, shining at the foot of her bed, those two pale, lemon-gray, liquid eyes. Why did they gaze at her that way? What did they want? They wanted something, those watery eyes that had not been extinguished the way the dog's barking had. How to extinguish them? Or why?

Her hands sought refuge in the inevitable crevice between her thighs. The magic little button, this time, responded — one could almost say that it came out to meet the caress of her sweet fingertips,

57

with which it had such a good understanding: the ring finger, the weakest, was also the most skilled in initiating the slow search for rhythm under the sheet, and her childhood game in the darkness of the tropics was recovered before those two chaste, twin moons that observed her—one moon very low in the sky along the horizon, another moon reflected in the hot ocean of the Caribbean night, two moons that were one—like those two eyes that made up a single gaze looking at her without comprehending, but moving beyond all comprehension: she and Archibaldo were like two moons that were two eyes, but only one moon, one gaze, one single pleasure. She wanted to incorporate the fantasy of Archibaldo into her solitary game, but, just as she was about to do so, the two moons were extinguished as the dog's eyelids covered them, and she fell asleep until the next morning.

When she awoke, warm and content, her first impulse, as every morning, was to ring for her maid Hortensia to bring in breakfast, and then decide on a dress to wear that day. She reached out a hand to do just that, and then saw Luna, already awake, curled up in the same position in the satin nest at the foot of her bed.

"Good morning, darling . . ." whispered Blanca.

And the dog, ecstatic—though not whining or barking, as though his whole relationship with the marquise were a thrilling secret—came to her, licking her face adoringly and sniffing at her with his tender, furry snout, his big tongue with its enormous buds licking her arms, her bare shoulders, her hands. Then Luna jumped to the floor and stared at her. The dog, now master of her attention, started to race around her room, arching his back, putting his head down and haunches up, tail raised, urging her to run and play with him. Blanca understood. Though she was a little fatigued from yesterday's excitement, she ran about with Luna, tumbling like a little girl over chairs, over tables ennobled by bronze, over the bed itself, while the dog chased her like he would chase a child, like the puppy he was, hiding behind furniture, and when they caught each other they embraced, lavishing each other with caresses, tumbling playfully onto the bed, as Blanca kissed his warm, furry jowl. Then, in the most unexpected moment of his cavorting, Luna raised a hind leg. Before Blanca could stop him, he urinated on the silk that covered the wall.

"Luna! Bad! Look what you've done! How am I going to explain this to Hortensia, who is so meddlesome?"

Then she had to stifle a scream so no one would hear her from outside: Luna, half-seated on the satin blanket of her bed, was defecating. Horrified, she ran in search of a newspaper page which she used to pick up the excrement and flush it down the toilet. She spent the rest of the morning trying to wash the soiled silk on the wall and her befouled bedspread, but without opening the door to her maid, who knocked several times to ask if she needed anything. Blanca told her no, that she just wanted to rest. She would get up a little later to go to her tennis class in Puerta de Hierro; tell Mario to have the Isotta Fraschini ready at eleven-thirty sharp.

When it was time to get dressed, she locked Luna in the bathroom, begging him to be quiet until she let him out again. Then Hortensia entered, bubbling over with the morning's gossip and carrying the immaculate tennis outfit — Blanca preferred to leave the house dressed so she wouldn't be tempted to go anywhere else after class — which the maid helped her don: the pleated little skirt, the white ribbon in the style of Suzanne Lenglen to keep her hair in place. While she was helping, Hortensia mentioned that, though she didn't know why, and she had noticed it a few times already in spring, there was a smell in Madame Marquise's room that morning, something neither pleasant nor unpleasant but in any case very different from the scent of other mornings. Blanca dismissed Hortensia. She let Luna out of the bathroom: he had to be good, she told him, and not make any noise. She would return at lunchtime to keep him company, and then, in the afternoon, when it was time, she would bring him to his owner's house, from which he never — not even out of love for her — should have run away.

When Blanca turned the key in the lock to her bedroom door, she told Hortensia not to try to enter while she was gone. All without giving any kind of explanation. She reflected on the advantages of power: the actions of the powerful, she thought to herself, are merely actions — it's not necessary to justify them, they simply are what they are. There was no reason for Hortensia to understand a thing. She was the boss: she could wipe the blackboard with a sponge to erase whatever she liked, whenever she liked. Hortensia had no right to make that sorrowful face, as if she were mortally offended.

6

IT WAS NEARLY TWELVE-THIRTY WHEN BLANCA LORIA AR-
rived at Puerta de Hierro and asked for Miss Merrington, her tennis
instructor. She was told that Miss Merrington had left a message
apologizing because she would be twenty minutes late that morning.
So British, Blanca thought—they would never understand that twenty
minutes is not late! She headed to the courts, which at that hour
were nearly deserted, mentally practicing her serve and delighted
with this image of yet another possible self: yes, she would suggest
to Archibaldo that he paint her just so, the archetype of the modern,
sporty girl, dressed all in white, in contrast with the lemon-gray water
of the Retiro pond in the background. It wasn't a bad idea. Her favorite
painting was *The Bathers* by Paul Chabas, and she pictured herself as
a bather, only clothed. It was, truly, an excellent idea . . . so excellent
that she felt an urge to run away to the painter's studio immediately.
But why "run away," and from whom? She had only to resolve to go,
she told herself, because what she needed right now was to know
what her body—that is, she herself—was capable of feeling. Miss
Merrington, tennis—those were paltry substitutes. The definitive way
to enjoy the sweet fullness of her existence was only in the penumbra
of Archibaldo's uncharted studio, lying nearly immobile, nearly dozing
off for hours and hours in his arms, while they caressed each other so
unhurriedly it was as if they had no objective beyond the delight of
that moment and that caress. Yes, she would go immediately. Why wait
for the appointed hour if he, like her, could do nothing the whole day

except prepare for the hour of their rendezvous? He must have sent Luna to her because her absence had driven him to desperation: the dog had not run away, he was Archibaldo's messenger.

From the other end of the courts, sitting at a low table under a striped umbrella, Tere Castillo called out her name as if they hadn't seen each other for ages. Blanca, feeling her breasts bounce under her light blouse, ran over to sit with her and a Frenchwoman who was so eccentric—not only was her hair cut *à la garçonne*, there was also the *chevalier* on her powerful pinkie, her thick voice, her tailored cashmere suit, her tie, her shoes with almost no heel—that, if she hadn't come escorted by Tere, who was always welcome everywhere in Madrid, she wouldn't have been allowed to set foot in Puerta de Hierro, in spite of the string of titles with which her friend introduced her. Blanca, on the other hand, was introduced simply as Casilda's *belle-fille*. With barely a glance toward Blanca and without a word to her, the Frenchwoman went on with a damning speech about the behavior of a certain friend in common, a speech that ended with the word *débauchée*.

"What does *débauchée* mean . . . ?" asked Blanca, as that word did not exist in the lexicon of the nuns in Nicaragua nor in Madrid.

The Frenchwoman halted her cascade of words and fixed Blanca with the needle of her gaze. Speaking directly to her for the first time, she replied: "C'est la manière dont vous couriez tout à l'heure, ma petite."

The conversation remained passionately stalled around the matter of Blanca's beauty: truly marvelous, especially blushing as she was now—so *primitive*—from the foreigner's flattery. Of course, she added, one could not expect the chic of the French from a Spanish woman, for no one who wore their hair like Blanca could aspire to such a high qualifier these days. It was of the utmost importance that Blanca cut her hair exactly like hers—and here she displayed her repulsive shaved neck—or like Clara Bow: madly *ébouriffée*. Definitely Clara Bow, said Tere. *À la garçonne*, said the Frenchwoman. And, to demonstrate, the lady took Blanca's hair and pulled it back, then made her look at herself in her compact mirror. Yes, it suited her, Blanca thought: like a beautiful little boy to whom the perverse Almanza could do certain things that she now knew existed. The strange Frenchwoman complained of her most recent lover: ". . . un jeune poète, beau, subtil, intelligent, cruel . . ."

Tere whispered into Blanca's ear that he had been a mere child, that it was inexplicable for him to be in love with this woman more than forty years old. The Frenchwoman looked at the other two in astonishment: "Mais c'est le décalage. Il faut absolument le décalage."

Luckily, in Spain that age difference wasn't so necessary, thought Blanca, rising. The less *décalage*, as with Archibaldo, the better; he had a few years on her, but there was no lack of symmetry there. That's why he had sent her the crepuscular eyes of his dog, which she was never going to return, keeping forever with her that part of Archibaldo embodied by his enamored pet, and forever those crepuscular eyes would light up her dreams. No. To hell with these Frenchwomen *à la garçonne*. To hell with tennis and Miss Merrington. She glanced at her Patek Philippe. Exclaiming that she was terribly late for an appointment, she bid them farewell, running to her car but making sure to mime the occasional serve, so that from beneath the umbrella where they were sipping sherry the two women could indulge in the pleasure of watching her personify that French word she did not know.

Mario started the car. He did not ask the marquise where she wanted him to take her, because it was natural that in that attire and at that hour, Blanca would only go one place: Castelló, almost at the corner of Lista, her house. But she was headed to Plaza de Chamberí, number eight. Just before they reached Cibeles, as Blanca knew the driver would turn toward Velázquez, his preferred route, she rolled down the glass between her and the Italian chauffeur and told him to turn left on Castellana. Mario's neck, shaved like the Frenchwoman's but younger and stronger, stiffened at this change to his routine. Hortensia was hopelessly in love with him; Blanca, who had sinister childhood memories of excessive familiarity with the help, did not encourage her to confide, though she did make certain concessions so that their days off coincided. When they reached Plaza Colón,

Blanca had him turn left on Génova. This time, Mario gave a start as he obeyed her. At Plaza Alonso Martínez she had him turn right on García Morato; the driver was visibly displeased, the tendons in his neck tightening. The habitual silence between the two of them became tense from the mere fact that the glass remained open and no longer kept them separate.

"Leave me here," said Blanca when they reached Chamberí.

"To what address are you going, Madame Marquise?"

"Leave me on this corner."

"You're going to get out like that . . . ?"

Since she did not have time to get angry at this admonition, Blanca merely dismissed him.

What if Archibaldo was not at his studio at that hour? She waited until the Isotta Fraschini had disappeared down Paseo del Cisne before starting her search for number eight. Pedestrians turned to look at her: this young woman, so beautiful, so astonishingly bold, her head bare and a Dunlop in her hand; she was an unusual sight in this neighborhood of fake flappers still stiff with passé corsets beneath their falsely risqué dresses, invariably and paradoxically headed to confession or returning from their visits to the poor. But she realized that even those women forgave her, because she was so lovely and provocative and looked too luminously happy for it not to be a pleasure to look at her. What did she care if she happened to meet an acquaintance? At most they would mention it to Casilda as an American eccentricity. And why should she care what Casilda thought? She was going to visit Archibaldo, with whom she was surely in love. Or with whom she would almost surely fall in love. He, a great artist, almost like Paul Chabas, was going to paint her a portrait of unrivaled excellence. Was this house number eight? Not bad, this charming and quite modern apartment building, with huge midrelief urns to either side of the doorway and stucco garlands around the windows. And she'd thought painters lived in garrets that reeked of frying oil, with those birdcages on all the balconies and clothes hung on lines, like you saw beyond Plaza Mayor!

Archibaldo's welcome was so polite that Blanca couldn't help but

64

feel some disappointment at the lack of an immediate sexual attack: yes, if only he had leapt upon her to possess her right there on the red rug of the dais where his models surely posed. The painter's simple courtesy was such, on the other hand, that it even held a hint of shyness, and Blanca was unsure whether she liked it or not. Or could it be embarrassment for having let the dog escape? She decided not to ask any questions about Luna: let him explain that it was all part of his great love for her.

It was one thirty, Blanca told him as she entered; she was only stopping by for a second. She wanted to take advantage of her morning at Puerta de Hierro for him to get a look at her in her white tennis outfit, to see if he liked the idea of painting her like that. Beaming at the notion, the painter declared it a daring innovation that would surely give people much to talk about. Blanca had gone over to the big window that opened over the treetops of the Plaza de Chamberí and stood gazing out at them. A few steps behind her, Archibaldo listened as she urbanely enthused over the studio's view, then came closer to share the sight with her, his body almost brushing against her back, his hand resting on the edge of the window so that, without touching the marquise, the curve of his arm contained her.

"Do you really like it . . . ?"

"I love it," she said, turning abruptly toward him so that she was practically cornered. He didn't move, only smiled. From so close up, she saw that the painter's eyes were not lemon-gray, because he had sent those eyes to her as a gift with his dog. She saw, rather, the black eyes from that first day smiling back at her. She could still feel a tingling on the backs of her knees from when he'd watched her flee up the stairs while the dog barked . . . and those white, white teeth surrounded by his irresistible black beard: she touched it.

"Scratchy!" she said.

Archibaldo caressed her head.

"Your hair, on the other hand, is not . . ."

"Your friend Tere Castillo," Blanca lied just to rile him up, "promised to bring me to the salon this week to cut it like Clara Bow's . . ."

Archibaldo, just barely leaning over, gave her a light kiss on the lips without taking his hand from the window. Then he drew his face away to smile at her again, intertwining his smile with hers. The shiver of pleasure that Blanca felt reached much deeper than if he had put his hand down her blouse to caress her breasts. The studio was flooded with the incomparable light of spring mornings in Madrid that turns everything to porcelain. Brightly colored cloths hung from the walls, and there was a voluminous blanket draped over a showy frame. She saw cushions, sketches, paintings turned toward the wall everywhere, in apparent disorder, but really, Blanca felt, it all had a sort of internal structure that corresponded to a certain sensitivity, a way of looking at life, that excited her. In the shadow of a dividing screen decorated with lilies and swallows, she spied a bed in a welcoming corner also adorned with a leopard skin and a vase of peacock feathers.

"No," he said, replying to something she seemed to have said a century ago, before the kiss, which had fully dispelled all memory of it.

"What ambiance this studio has!" Blanca exclaimed.

"I saw Tere Castillo go by this morning," said Archibaldo, a bit of bewitching tension still lingering between them. "From this very spot where we are now I saw her with all her plumage and she looked up, but I hid, fearing she would get the idea to come up and demand I go for a walk with her. I don't go out with her anymore. The last time, she made me go with her to Gran Vía. She was dressed in red and yellow and looked just like the flag, everyone stood to attention before her. I did what I could to strike her colors, but it was no use, people started to walk like in a parade . . . because of course, Tere's colors cannot be struck . . ."

Blanca burst out laughing, so caught up in pure amusement that she scarcely managed to squeeze her thighs together to keep from peeing herself—a small tragedy that had happened to her before, when she laughed so much at the opening of Arniches's play, *Mecachis, qué guapo soy!* Seeing her enjoyment, Archibaldo went on:

"The worst was when we crossed the street, because the police stopped traffic, and Tere, of course, started waving happily to everyone as if it were the most natural thing in the world . . ."

Blanca was faint from laughter and had no choice but to collapse against his arm. Archibaldo's hand, then, left the window frame to encircle her waist gently with his arm, and his other hand, as she caressed his beard, sought out her hot neck beneath her hair. Blanca fastened herself to his mouth. She kissed him so long and so sweetly right where they were, surrendering so unhurriedly to that elemental caress that it was like reading only the title of a book from which you can infer something of its contents. They had their whole lives, entire volumes, ahead of them: this kiss triggered the first spring of the mechanism of pleasure that would make them — as all novelists assure us — vibrate in unison.

Eons later, at the end of that sweet kiss that seemed to have lit another light in the studio, Archibaldo and Blanca put their arms around one another's waists: he was going to show her his paintings. An enormous group of variegated Madrileños were set upon easels, filling one whole section of the studio with clamor and flowers. The strong, simple features sketched on several canvases in paint thinned with turpentine awaited the return of their models to sit for the painter. There was a platform with an armchair — for the model, Blanca supposed — and a drawing pad on the seat of one chair with another facing it. Archiboldo picked up some charcoal and magically, in a mere second, transferred Blanca's face to the paper, thus seizing control of her very being, as native peoples feared would happen when someone took their photograph. Blanca's heart — why not? — beat furiously. How was it possible? How was all this possible, this heat on her waist from that hand that she wanted to stay there forever, free of hurry or fear? How was it possible to smell without shame her rising feminine fragrance as it subtly overpowered the atmosphere and permeated everything? At one point, when she was particularly enthusiastic about celebrating a painting — which was easy, because they were all very pretty — he pulled her to him and kissed her. That initial disappointment when he hadn't fallen upon her immediately to devour her like a wolf vanished: this long prologue to the inevitable was in itself a form of pleasure, which later on would be easily tuned to a different pitch.

Suddenly, Archibaldo announced that he was hungry. Perhaps they could eat something, first . . . so as not to interrupt, well, the session to come. Yes, perhaps, she agreed. Then, why not go down to the tavern to eat something light. She said that under no circumstances would she go dressed as she was. He urged her not to be silly: her beauty and youth—finally, someone had the good sense not to include her title and fortune!—in any clothes, and especially the ones she was wearing now, would cause a sensation anywhere she went.

"What mad things this man is making me do!" she exclaimed.

But she *was* hungry, so she went with him.

The entrance of the marquise of Loria, smiling, hatless and dressed in all white, into the tavern El Bilbaíno with its throngs of vociferating men—workers, employees, scions, whatever they were, it didn't matter: they were all the same because they were young and drinking and eating and laughing and arguing—was a crowning moment. The crowd parted to allow for the couple to reach the bar, clapping Archibaldo on the back, asking him where he had found this angel they all wanted to pray to and what revue was she to appear in so they could buy up all the theater tickets, and they were enchanted with Blanca when she replied that tickets weren't for sale but she was giving them away, and they were amused and respectful because Blanca was with Archibaldo, friend or acquaintance of nearly all of them; they offered tumbler after tumbler, which the couple drank, and they ate a few things as well, until Blanca, looking around and seeing so many faces entranced with her person, felt capable of satisfying them all if they were to close the place down right now and undress her. Archibaldo, taller and more dapper than the others in his big black hat, soon began to say goodbye to his friends, who wouldn't let him pay because they wanted to fête the angel whom the painter had stolen from heaven. Opening a path through the masses gathered around them, Blanca started to leave, blowing kisses with her fingertips and accepting this and that very intentional touch to her delicious behind; the crowd was singing a song in the couple's honor when they emerged onto the street and went up in the slow elevator that took an age to reach their floor. Tipsy from so many tumblers, he grabbed her roughly and kissed her on the mouth, and although the gadget's grille did not supply privacy for such displays of affection, he put his hand under Blanca's skirt to find again the silk of her hips. She pulled her mouth away to apologize: "I had to wear them today, because you can't play tennis without . . ."

The frustration they both felt ended when, upon closing the apartment door behind them, he led her to the bed.

"Take off your clothes . . ." he whispered, while he did the same, tossing, like her, all his clothing onto on the rug, folding back the screen to open the bed to the gold and green and transparent light that shone in through the window panes, illuminating the supple undulations of Blanca's body, already laid out with half-closed eyes and damp eyelids, which was a sight he wanted to luxuriate in.

"How pretty you are!"

Blanca opened her eyes to smile at him from the bed.

"So are you."

And it was true: the slender elegance of his muscles, torso, and legs governed by nerves controlling each tendon: "So strong and thin . . . like Paavo Nurmi . . ."

Then, in bed, all the skin of one pressed up against all the other's skin, they gave themselves over to the world's very first embrace. It was all elementary, free of strategy, just the joyful spontaneity of pleasure, his mouth kissing hers in a thousand different ways, their intertwined legs cool despite the excitement, arms an imaginative sequence of knots, hands, fingers seeking out coccyx and neck and venturing further, to where the vegetation began. She would stay, she decided, and it didn't matter what anyone said, not just tonight, but tomorrow, and maybe the day after, and after . . . and after that, until they were drained of delight, who knows when, or if it was even possible to drain it all away. Her breasts had taken on an entirely new life, like two little animals ready and willing not to devour but rather to graze on or drink from the caresses her companion was lavishing upon them, and all of her was open though he had not yet possessed her. That was what she wanted. Because all of those preliminaries, these explorations of her armpits which she knew were so lovely, with his lips or his sex itself, all of it was forming a sort of plait of caresses, a natural crescendo, one braided turn leading into another turn on the other side, and so love grew and lengthened out and was an infinitely coherent thing. Neither of them felt the other's weight above or suffocation below, and both were active, hungry, dedicated: waists, bellies, hairs tangled in one's damp pubis which was the reflection of the other's small triangular night, until after what seemed like hours and hours of caresses and searches and discoveries, she lay face up, and he, who looked immense and ready atop her, obeyed her instantly when she practically shouted at him, for it was the only thing left: "Now, my love, now . . ."

And Archibaldo fell onto the sweet, glowing, soft body that he had been smelling and caressing and savoring, penetrating her to depths she would never have believed she could contain until his thrusting insisted upon her awareness of them, far beyond the little button but including it, and she responded to his slow vertical rhythm with a circular one that complemented it, supporting it and adding another meaning upon joining in with it, both mouths sharing the same breath, both perspiring the same sweat, their distinct anatomies transformed for that instant into a single animal that sought out two distinct pleasures that were but one, a beast, loving but frenzied, that was assembled by the arc of Blanca's thighs around Archibaldo's hips, thighs that squeezed him, that urged him on and demanded more delirium until he felt he could explode whenever she wanted him to, after a century of pleasure that was drawn out longer and longer, his mouth on those tresses that would not be cut off because he asked her not to, her blushing ear entirely inside his mouth with his tongue tasting it, his tongue, yes, probing, yes, there, yes, until Blanca, crazed, murmured: "Now . . ."

And he agreed: "Now . . ."

And when he said it he exploded, shuddered, filled her, and she, delirious, joined her spasm to his. Then an independent and prolonged pleasure opened up and flowered in Blanca, because Archibaldo stayed solid inside her until she had savored the last echo of that drawn-out pleasure that would never happen the same way again. At least, that's what Blanca dreamed: as she dozed with him sunk beside her into sleep that would perhaps last no more than a minute, if he ever fell fully asleep . . . she tried to make love to him again, but he melted down like Paquito, he died like Don Mamerto, he arched his left eyebrow like Almanza . . . but no: Archibaldo was asleep, his cheek right there beside her own.

Asleep? Like her? Caressing him—was he only feigning sleep so she would have her way with him?—she devoured him with kisses while he lay inert, pretending, deliciously passive even though he was again so hard that she mounted him, watching as a smile spread little by little across his lips under his beard, as she, little by little, sank down astride him. When he touched bottom, she felt a shiver animate his inert body as he sensed the full profundity of Blanca, who shivered simultaneously—and wanted to see him shiver again. Again, she rose up, freeing Archibaldo, to repeat from the start that marvelous process of gradual devouring, and again, and again, to drive him mad, to wake him up . . . until she realized that Archibaldo could scarcely stand it, her body affixed there and gyrating, but with him unmoving, exactly as she wanted him, though, through barely open eyes, he delighted in the spectacle of her small breasts bouncing, in the dance of those tips that he wanted to bite, in the wonderful fold of Blanca's hip joining his own hip to become the wonderful bicephalous and hermaphroditic animal of shared pleasure . . . As she grew closer to ecstasy, she leaned over so the tips of her breasts brushed against his chest, electrifying him, the four nipples active and sensitive and crazed with sensation as she sped up her rhythm atop that man who played dead from the pleasure she was giving him, the quartet of sensitized nipples that finally he could not resist, and, embracing her, pressed her to him, and she squeezed her body and squeezed his body in a frenetic orgasm that laid them both out flat, panting.

The awakening, this time, was slow, perhaps because their sleep lasted longer. They woke up already in the midst of caresses that they had apparently been lavishing on one another in dreams . . . and they explored their moles and told each other the stories of their small scars, laughing over hairs that sprouted in the wrong places, giving island names to certain red spots on their skin caused by amorous excesses that had perhaps caused a little pain, but pain that had helped them reach pleasure and had merged with it, no, no, yes, but it didn't hurt, don't be silly, but look at the marks from my teeth here . . . how can it not have hurt you . . . yes, my love, I did hurt you, you don't mind? And this rough mole, could it be cancer? though perhaps it would be strange to have cancer on the waist. And the wonder of the four nipples that added fire to the fire below: they were meticulously examined, recognized, tasted. Until Blanca saw the twilight invading the room and said, "It feels a little cold . . ."

Archibaldo leapt from the bed and lit the kerosene stove, which he placed near but not too near the bed. They started to tell each other things, and she talked about Nicaragua. Why Nicaragua, she wondered as she spun her tale, when she didn't like it at all and was so happy here in Madrid? Her tiresome, envious sisters, especially Charo, who was closest to Blanca in age and looked like her, though she was much darker, and the dark-skinned women of her childhood, and the moon over the Caribbean. But Archibaldo didn't react the way she expected him to, mourning the dog's escape upon hearing his name (*Luna*, moon). Why did he keep quiet? What secret was he keeping from her? She wasn't about to ask. If he really loved her, then, without her asking, he had to explain Luna's inexplicable — to everyone but her, and surely to him — absence. And him? So much to say: he struck her as a man of mystery, talent, wisdom. She listened to him talk about his master Anglada Camarasa, who was the greatest genius Spanish painting had ever produced, and to whom he owed his profession and his technique. One afternoon, when Archibaldo was no more than a boy, Anglada sent him to deliver a message to the house of a Cuban beauty who was a little mature, but still very famous for her splendid breasts and her exuberant persona. When she saw the young emissary enter her salon, she mistook him for the master, referring to him as a genius, a poet of color, master of the rainbow, and she embraced him, touching him, plying him with compliments such that young Archibaldo couldn't interrupt the torrent of praise to inform the lavish lady of her mistake. Such was her frenetic enthusiasm for the false Anglada Camarasa that in a fit of passion she took a lovely breast from her plunging neckline and placed it in the boy's hand, saying, "Here, take this, all yours; it's the best thing I have, and I'm very pleased to offer it to you . . ."

And she stuffed her enormous breast into young Archibaldo's pocket.

"What?"

"That's right, here, in my breast pocket."

When they looked at each other, they both burst out laughing at the same time. Blanca was choked with a peal of laughter so crazed she couldn't stifle it, she lost control of her body and felt, spreading out under her naked behind, a hot puddle she could not hold back as she thought about that big breast in the little pocket, and her laughter only increased. She blushed in spite of the hilarity, and clung to him so as not to feel the shameful wetness, so he wouldn't see her red face. Exhausted from their laughter, he touched the wetness with his hand.

"No," said Blanca. "It's dirty . . ."

"Why dirty . . . ?"

"I don't know, those are disgusting things that poor people do . . ."

And he pulled away from Blanca's arms and put his bearded face up to the hot stain left by her loss of control and kissed it tenderly, lightly. She pulled him on top of her. The games of love began again until the big window darkened and they were both dozing, with the light of the street lamps illuminating the treetops and the glow of the kerosene stove filling the room with secretive whispers, and she lit up a perfumed Miss Blanche. Later, Archibaldo asked her to pose naked for him, and she was happy to oblige, though she begged him not to draw her face so that no one could identify her. But she felt such pride, such pleasure at seeing herself in those pretty sketches she posed for again and again without ever growing tired, that during one long, drawn-out pose, with one arm behind her head and a knee flexed—like *The Source*, by Ingres, said Archibaldo, who was very cultured—she could not hold back an orgasm, solitary but provoked by Archibaldo's eyes examining her most intimate parts, an orgasm in which she didn't want to include her lover: she would rather keep it a secret.

Why not, if he didn't share with her the secret reason for the dog's absence?

Then, above all because she felt a little cold, she put her tennis outfit back on, and, with racket in hand and her arm raised high, displaying the remarkable beauty of her underarm, while Archibaldo told her more stories about Anglada Camarasa, about Moreno Carbonero, about Pons Arnau and other painters whose names meant nothing to her, but which she liked to hear, she let the artist draw countless sketches for her portrait . . . but Blanca didn't really like any of them. She was debating whether to tell him or not, when the doorbell rang.

"Who could it be?" asked Blanca, startled.

"It doesn't matter. I'm a professional. Don't you see? I am painting a portrait of the marquise of Loria in sports clothes, which will be shown to great acclaim."

It was Tere Castillo, now without the Frenchwoman. She struggled to hide her surprise at finding Blanca on the model's platform in a tennis pose. Her scrutinizing eyes sought out signs that, luckily, Blanca and Archibaldo had erased from the bed and washbasin. She hugged Blanca and smothered her in kisses, as was her theatrical habit every time they met.

"But my dear Dowager Marquise, I had no idea . . . ! You and your little secrets. Careful, that can be dangerous." She went over to admire the tennis sketches. "My, these are just fabulous! How original, how modern—an important portrait in tennis clothes! Truly fabulous, I swear! Why don't you paint one just like it of me, Archie? Though I don't know how to play tennis, and I don't look a thing like Lilí Álvarez, of course. I think with my build I'd be a more like the Statue of

Liberty with my arm held up like that. What a laugh! Have you already started on the portrait of Paquito that Don Mamerto commissioned? Where are the wings?"

"The marquise came by for just that reason, to see if they had brought them to me and to discuss the portrait, and that's when I decided to paint a portrait of her in sports clothes."

"Let's see. These are the sketches of him? You haven't made much progress . . ."

What if she recognizes my naked body? Blanca thought in terror. Impossible. Her body was that of any young girl, any plump and tender model . . . No. But what had Tere come for? To snoop . . . ? What right did she have over Archibaldo's time and work? Were they having an affair? So artificial, the way she addressed Blanca with her full title . . . Did he have affairs with all the women, all the famous ladies who posed for him? Was that why—and for being so handsome and charming—his name was becoming fashionable among women like Tere Castillo? How did Tere know about Paquito's wings, when the portrait had only been ordered yesterday? Archibaldo hadn't even mentioned Paquito's portrait to her. So many unknown things in this room, things Archibaldo hid from her—it was hard to forgive him, she thought furiously, for having spent the whole day with her and still stubbornly refusing to mention Luna's disappearance—and they were things she refused to untangle! Very well. Even if Tere was having an affair with Archibaldo, she had her own with Almanza. She had decided not to go to her date with him tomorrow night, but every decision can be revoked. *Oh Archie, these are just fabulous, I swear!* The gall! If contact with her divine flesh killed him, all the better: let him pay the consequences. She glanced at her Patek Philippe. Oh! she cried, picking up her Dunlop. It was very late. She had to leave immediately. She would let him know when she could come again . . .

"What . . . you're leaving?" Archibaldo cried.

"Yes, I'd prefer to put an end to the session, I'm tired," she replied, thinking of Luna, of his calm, liquid eyes waiting for her in her bedroom. He, at least, was constant; tomorrow, Almanza wouldn't even pretend to be, and there was comfort in that, too. But she wasn't about to leave Tere here, either. She told her that, since it was Mario's day off, he wouldn't be waiting for her, and in that outfit, at that hour, it was better not to show her face outside. Could Tere drop her off at home . . . ?

The goodbyes were brief, not to say curt, which made Tere raise a suspicious eyebrow. They got into the coupe that she drove herself—certain annals of Madrid still remember with affectionate nostalgia that Tere Castillo was one of the first society ladies who drove her own car, like a man—and they headed toward the Loria palazzo, which after all was only a few blocks away, on the other side of Castellana.

Blanca didn't listen to what Tere was saying. She didn't want to hear. Let her say what she liked against Archibaldo, though every accusation came preceded by a "though of course, he's just a ducky boy . . ." And why was she speaking so highly of her cousin Almanza? Blanca didn't want to hear anything about anyone. The next week, after leaving her affairs in order with the Mamertos, she would start planning a trip to Nicaragua, where she would disappear for a long time. As gifts for her horrid sisters she would bring nothing but her cast-off dresses. If this little painter wanted to play at being Don Juan, let him find someone else. Now Tere was listing all the arch-frivolous women, like her, who considered the painter to be a real darling. Tomorrow she would go without fail to Chez Alphonse to cut her hair *à la garçonne*: she couldn't wait to hear what that "ducky boy" would have to say about such an innovation. And she got out at the front door of her house without even saying goodbye to Tere.

Her servants were visibly worried when they opened the door for her. Seeing her come in, a weepy Hortensia came running down the stairs. What had she been doing all day dressed in sports clothes? A good thing she was with Señorita Tere, who was a saint! Blanca went up the steps of her house, as slow and indifferent as if she were climbing Palace stairs dragging a long train behind her. She could have at least left the keys to her bedroom so it could be tidied, Hortensia chided her . . . In any case, she'd have it done in a jiffy . . .

"None of that," the marquise stopped her with a hand on the locked doorknob. "I shall not dine tonight. You go to bed. Or rather, you have the night off . . . go on, go out with Mario. I'll call for you tomorrow morning when I want breakfast. Goodnight."

And she shut the door in her maid's face. The two moons looked at her in the darkness from their satin nest at the foot of the bed. They were two clearly defined orbs, gold-gray, the gray of twilight at that hour in Retiro Park when it's hard to tell a human figure from a withered tree or a figment of the imagination. There was something sacramental about those two fixed spheres, and it brought back the serenity that half an hour ago she'd believed lost forever. She would have liked to spend the rest of her days in that darkness, watched by those two distinct moons that constituted one single gaze. But to enter any further she needed to turn on the light.

When she did, she let out a shriek. Everything was destroyed, the bedclothes mangled, the armchairs gutted, her brocade dressing gown torn to shreds, her slippers bitten, chewed, mutilated, everything in shambles, a filthy world that had nothing at all to do with her . . . such a smell of urine and excrement. Next to the bed, though, the dish in which she'd served the dog's meat looked clean. Slowly, never taking his eyes off of her as if he wanted to hypnotize poor Blanca, Luna, all gray, all flannel, all tendon and muscle and precise movements, got down from the bed, and without ceasing to look at her for one second, he went over to the empty dish. With the transparent moons of his tranquil eyes on Blanca, he started to lick the already cleaned dish, voraciously, and she, defeated, dropped her tennis racket onto the ruined rug. She would not go down to find him food. Why, when he had behaved so poorly? She had the right to be angry, and to retaliate. Even if the dog died of hunger, and she did too.

She locked the door from inside. She saw that powerful people — people like her, for example — do, in the end, have to give explanations. But how to explain this? She had to clarify it for herself before she could give an account to the staff . . . though it was very strange that Hortensia, who stuck her nose into everything, had not mentioned hearing any noise coming from her room. But it was more than that.

77

What was she trying to lock up, by locking a crazed dog alone in her room for an entire day? What would it have cost her to leave him with her gardener, for example, out in the yard? Who was stopping her from owning a big gray puppy—a Weimaraner, as Archibaldo had explained the first time they'd strolled together through Retiro Park—an elegant dog, expensive, young, and friendly? Those vacant moons looked at her as the large tongue, whose buds knew the taste of her satiny arms so well, licked the dish . . . On fear-filled nights, the mestiza women of her childhood had pointed to two identical moons on the horizon to soothe her. But why had Luna unleashed this domestic calamity—Luna, her beloved dog, whom, she now realized, she had spent the whole day missing, especially his eyes suspended on the very horizon of her imagination? Yes, you're hungry, dog who is more intelligent than men, and more sensitive. You want to convince me to go down and get you some meat. But first you have to justify your destruction, your filth, your hatred, your violence. It was necessary to make him understand that she had no meat for him now. She went over to the dog as he licked the dish, and, before petting him, she opened her hands in a gesture of impotence. She shrugged her shoulders to convey her lack of nourishment: she did not have meat.

The dog, growling very low, leapt at her, pushing her down onto the filthy tatters he'd made of her bed, and started to bite off the tennis clothes that had garnered so much admiration during the day, shredding them and slobbering on them. The weight of his powerful paws held her down on the bed, face up in a vertigo of terror that made it impossible to catch her breath and fight back: she could only let herself be stripped naked by those bloodthirsty fangs, and be burned by that searing nose, and be suffocated by that stinking, panting muzzle. She couldn't scream. She lay nearly unconscious under the beast that was tearing off not only the white dress and pullover, but also her blouse, skirt, underwear, bra, until she was completely naked and moaning. For a second she thought—without fear, because she saw those two drops of transparent moonlight looking at her—that the dog was going to rape her: it would at least have given her peace of mind of a sort, to understand a motive, to have access to an explanation, a shared instinct . . . but it wasn't that. What was it? And realizing that she would never know, she felt herself rocked by a ferocious shiver that culminated in an orgasm of terror under that body she could not satisfy with her sex that was so very capable of satiating — even killing — anyone.

Then, once Luna understood that Blanca had given him everything, he seemed to be appeased. Those who are truly the masters of a situation have no need to be cruel or despotic: those pale, still eyes were enough. And as Blanca tumbled vertiginously into her nightmare, Luna gathered up the tatters of the white tennis outfit belonging to the little marquise of Loria, making them into a sort of nest on the floor, then curled up on it to sleep.

Blanca was falling fully asleep. Luna, his lemon-gray eyes so incomprehensibly devoid of intensity, so empty, shining in a different way than the crystal, than the teardrop chandelier and the silver objects and the bronze furniture in the nuptial bedroom redecorated after Paquito's death as though for another wedding, sat staring at her all night long, meaning to keep her forever in the orbit of his pale twin satellites.

7

THE FIRST THING BLANCA SAW, UPON WAKING WITH HER
neglected hands covering her face, was that her lovely fingernails
were a disaster: rough, the polish chipped, her cuticles uneven and
hangnailed. This meant she would need to call Hortensia in to give
her a manicure if she planned to appear at Almanza's house as she
wanted to: made into a dream. But she wasn't going to call Hortensia,
or anyone else. She was going to remain alone, a prisoner of her own
will in a room devastated by that dog who knew more about her than
she did herself, until it was time to leave, so that Almanza could try
to fulfill his promise and remove the curse.

Her beautiful room was every bit as devastated — or more — than
her poor nails, but somehow, she couldn't care less: if she did not ac-
quiesce to the terror, nothing had happened here. This, after all, was
her house. She had the right to decide which things that happened in
it were real, and which, kept quiet, absolutely did not happen.

From her perspective — the sheet pulled over her head, because
she didn't want to see a thing — it was merely a question of calling
in upholsterers and woodworkers, asking them for an estimate, and
handing them a check once the work was finished, having previously
dispatched the dog to one of her most remote holdings — in Ex-
tremadura, for example — where she had never set foot. Let no one
in her service dare to even raise an eyebrow in surprise upon seeing
the destruction: that would mean their immediate termination. She
was not willing to tolerate censure. Questions, even less. And not from

Casilda, either. She would take care of Casilda, who, once she sensed Blanca's strong and renewed attitude of invulnerability, would not dare stick her nose in. For the moment it was necessary to confine herself to the serious problem of her fingernails, so as not to think about the bedroom that stank like a zoo cage or the sordid Archibaldo problem: to merely hold, suspended in her imagination, the quietude of two pale stars gazing at her.

But Luna was not looking at her. Restless but not wild, Luna was giving the occasional scratch to the wood frame of the window that opened out over the garden. Let him scratch! In that chaos, what did a few marks on the windowsill matter, when his claws had already wholly shredded the silk wall covering? Anyway, she had the power to control everything: Hortensia would not come up until Blanca called her, they had agreed on that the night before. No one had permission to come up to this floor. She herself, through the orders she gave, was her own protector. But what did that dog want now, to make it scratch so insistently at the window, with such purpose, such calculation? It was late, perhaps past lunchtime, or even teatime; she looked at her Patek Philippe under the translucent sheet that covered her head. Since she hadn't wound it, it was showing four in the morning. Or four in the afternoon? It was possible that she had in fact wound it unconsciously at some point when she was talking to herself under the spell of Luna's eyes. These expensive watches with such aristocratically discreet mechanisms — one never knew whether they had stopped or not. After a moment she realized that Luna had managed to scratch the window open, so that light streamed into the room, and the dog, standing on his hind legs, was looking out at the garden as if he were waiting for someone or wanted to go out. Would the gardener, or the porter — in sum, the help — see his face from outside? Would the fullness of those lunar eyes shine out in the light of day? And so what if the servants *did* see him? Whether they saw him or not, they must never ask for an explanation or question her at all. Unless she decided to lie to them and say she had just bought this beautiful Weimaraner puppy to join their household. But that was a concession she was not willing to make. What could she explain, when her shoulders still ached where the dog had placed his giant paws to immobilize her on the bed? He didn't rape her, because it wasn't about that . . .

Blanca leapt from her bed, ran to the bathroom and locked herself in without looking either at Luna or the filth of her bedroom. In the clean, fresh bathroom and the adjoining dressing room, it was possible to think of a world in which the dog's indecipherable eyes did not yet exist. And Blanca Loria spent two, three hours locked in there, carefully, obsessively doing her nails, and finally sinking into a long bath of Clark's salts. Then she rubbed herself with flower-scented milk, and finished off by choosing and donning her most chic item — chiffon, she thought to herself — of flowered muslin with a gypsy swirl of a skirt. When she was ready, she emerged: Luna, overcome by her beauty, went still, merely sitting down to admire her. It was late. The Patek Philippe had not stopped. The open window was dark. Yes: the hour when the phalaena fly.

She told Hortensia and the porter that she would return very late that night, and that no one should wait up for her. But, she warned, no one she be so bold as to go up to her room in her absence. The maid — who clearly hadn't slept, either out of worry or because she'd made the most of a night with Mario — said yes, Madame Marquise; no, Madame Marquise; yes, Madame Marquise, never daring to ask why she couldn't go up and what had made those strange noises that she must have heard. All as it should be. Blanca told the driver to take her to the count of Almanza's house. That short trip through Madrid to Calle Ruiz de Alarcón helped her forget it all, to wipe the slate clean, one might say, and become like new as she decided that tonight, she would sleep at the Ritz. Tomorrow she would call in at the Mamertos and have them sell off the palazzo so she would never see it again, nor her clothes: she would buy all new things. Nor would she see her staff, so there would be no need to explain a thing to them.

Almanza was waiting for her, this time in a Cossack's blouse of bottle-green satin. As soon as Blanca entered, he started to kiss her with the same yearning rictus of passion as the first time, which now she did not find ridiculous at all. On the contrary, Almanza seemed to possess something Archibaldo lacked: since the count did not feel any true pleasure either in the kiss or the caress, the love he manifested was a representation dedicated to her alone, since his role was merely executor, and left the whole spectrum of pleasure free for her to consume.

This time, Almanza had the ritual champagne chilled and ready, and he uncorked it with the same refined technique that he showed and, in some slightly tedious way that she still couldn't figure out, even emphasized in everything he did well. Almanza moved the guitar from the divan to sit beside Blanca among the cushions and observe as her *scarlet, cursed-blood lips sipped champagne from fine baccarat* while they chatted a bit. Oh yes, what a great poet, Darío! He, on the other hand, had been born in Huelva, he told her, where his ancestors had been caciques since time immemorial; he wasn't trying, certainly, to compete with the divine Rubén from her Nicaraguan lands, but in Atlantic Andalusia — and here he picked up the guitar — the popular poetry of the fandango was not, at times, any less exciting or heartfelt than that of her compatriot. Blanca begged him to play something, to sing. He excused himself as he tried out a few notes, saying that he didn't have much of a voice. But then he intoned, with no small amount of flair:

> *A butterfly is taking flight*
> *On the wing toward a streetlamp's light.*
> *Anyone who may fail to learn*
> *to love well, and to risk the height,*
> *only attempts to spare the burn . . .*

Blanca clapped, very impressed. She downed her whole glass of champagne and asked for more and more as she let him kiss her arms and décolleté. Then — really, just to get him off of her — she begged him to sing another fandango. He obliged. Did she want to hear a bawdy one? Bawdy . . . ? Yes, bawdy . . . but very, very bawdy . . . Why not? And to please her, the count sang out:

As the strawberry fountain flowed
My lady sipped out on the hunt
And high on the Guillena Road
I gave a good suck to her . . .

"Oh!" she cried, pretending to be shocked. "My goodness . . . !"
And the count of Almanza concluded, chivalrously:

. . . and oh, what a treasure to hunt . . .

"How wonderful, Almanza! In addition to being handsome and a
great man, you're also a great artist!" Blanca happily exclaimed.
"And a great . . . ?"
"Lover?"
"Say it . . . say it, my love . . . I burn to hear it from your lips!"
He didn't give her a chance to say it, for he began to kiss her. She,
meanwhile, jabbed a freshly manicured nail into the Cossack's blouse,
right at the nipple, but Almanza didn't react with a shiver the way
Archibaldo would have. She sipped more champagne and then—why
not?—conceded:
"Yes: a great lover."
A humble Almanza retorted:
"Also a popular tradition of my homeland . . ."
Kissing her again, he declared that he was going to make her feel
every imaginable emotion as long as she was strong enough to bear
them, to not blush, to be a truly civilized woman and not be surprised
or scandalized by anything. She declared herself completely amenable.
Between caresses that came to bore Blanca a bit, they finished the
bottle of champagne. Then, standing up, Almanza told her he was
going into his bedroom. After ten minutes, she was to enter too, naked.
"How embarrassing!" Blanca cried.
"The lights will be off."
"All right."
"You will find everything your heart could desire."

When she entered Almanza's darkened bedroom, for a moment she thought—hoped—she would find Luna's luminous eyes guiding her toward the object of her longing. But no. Almanza's voice softly calling to her was her only lodestar. She walked closer to where she knew the bed was. The count's hands touched her, made her lie down beside his muscled body, also naked, and he wrapped her in his arms. But this time, in spite of the classic champagne, Blanca's body did not respond: she remained utterly cold—though she extended the rudimentary courtesy of pretending otherwise—uninterested, not even thinking about Archibaldo, or thinking, rather, that the exact same thing would be happening if he, and not Almanza, were caressing her. It was as if something within her had been permanently used up, or was somewhere else, perhaps on a cold and distant star. Almanza, who had too much experience not to realize Blanca wasn't responding, murmured sweet obscenities into her ear, snippets of fandangos that were absolutely unrepeatable. But it was like he was saying it all from very far away, addressing an auditorium that didn't include her. Finally, fed up, before she allowed Almanza to sink into her, Blanca asked: "Is this the promised excitement?"

"No," replied Almanza. "This is . . ."

And, turning over in the bed, he placed her where he had just been, and took Blanca's previous spot. Immediately, she could tell there was another naked person lying very still beside her in the bed. Then, as if a switch had been flipped, her entire body began to burn again, to feel again. This, then, was the surprise?

Well . . . of course, it would depend on who this other person was.

The body beside her did not hesitate to make itself known: in the first instant, she thought it seemed merely a softer body, as though with too much flesh, that was embracing and kissing her with strange warmth. A woman! Startled during that first half second, she then felt that her very fright would act as a stimulus, making it easy for her to respond to the caresses of those fingers, so soft and so knowledgeable—much more so than those of any man—as they toyed with her overstimulated nipples, while behind her, Almanza supplied what by nature the woman could not. No one spoke. But they adopted a rhythm, the three of them, stimulus and response and response to that other stimulus that was a response that demanded another response that was itself another stimulus ... the unknown woman exploring Blanca's entire body with her tongue until she reached her vertex, where she executed with the most impeccable mastery what Almanza's fandango had promised, until she made her *feel* again; Blanca exaggerated her response, because at the end of the day she was a polite girl, the daughter of diplomats, who didn't want to offend anyone. But she was only feeling. There was no delight, she thought, a little bored, because to her, these things between women didn't rise to the category of love — was it the same between two men? — and it wasn't, to her, what some people with a pedantically scientific lexicon would call a "sexual relationship." Tension was lacking, or something else — something at least in her case, since she'd rather not generalize: it was like the pale reflection of the naughty games of her childhood, between little girl cousins made to spend the night in the same bedroom because there weren't enough beds for the newest visitors to the hacienda, already overflowing with guests and family — games that were expiated with the very light punishment of two days without coconut candy when they were caught. The other thing was serious, real. Suddenly, Almanza turned on the bedside light.

"Look ..." he murmured.

Before he'd gotten the word out, in the first instant of light, before she could even put a possessive hand over her breasts, Blanca recognized Tere Castillo's malevolent smile. Immediately she scrambled over Almanza, who tried to hold her back, and leapt from the bed to Tere's desperation; Tere called her name in the sweetest intonations her booming voice could muster, which mingled with Almanza's pleas as he tried to entice her by making a show of biting his cousin's nipples.

"Come," Tere urged. "Don't be silly, my love, we won't say a word to Casilda and we'll have fun just the three of us."

Blanca, who had decided to leave tout de suite, revoked this decision when she realized that she could learn many things in this company, though not precisely the things Almanza and Tere proposed to teach her. Tere went on pleading with her between sighs of pleasure from the count's caresses:

"Don't go to Archibaldo, beautiful, he doesn't know how to make love like we do . . . he believes love means marriage and children, he's a yokel, a gimlet . . . a terrible painter, and he's made his name just by painting all the well-heeled ladies thinner than they are and their pearls fatter, just how they like it . . . you, my darling, no . . . you deserve something better . . . come . . . don't leave . . ."

"I'm a little cold and it's getting late . . . and Casilda could get angry if she found out . . . I'm afraid . . ."

Almanza laughed. "Casilda? Oh please, Casilda is so frigid you catch a cold just sitting next to her . . ."

To which Tere added: "Look, deary, just so you know: Casilda and . . ."

"Zip it, you fool," her cousin Almanza stopped her. "You'll ruin everything . . ."

Tere, nearly hysterical as she pushed Almanza aside, sat up on the bed and told him:

"Let me put the cards on the table once and for all, so she'll understand. Don't you see she's in love with Archibaldo and we could lose everything, with his obsession about having children . . . ?"

Blanca allowed Tere to caress her thighs and tell her how they were soft as silk, an observation she had already heard on more interesting occasions, while Almanza ran for reinforcements in the form of more champagne. But Blanca was surprised to find that what she had just ascertained about Archibaldo's behavior, and which was in essence what she was interested in finding out, did not move her in the slightest, neither for better nor for worse, and that if she thought about what all these characters could offer her—aside from some fun—there was simply nothing there. Almanza filled their glasses, and the three of them drank. Another glass in, amid caresses in which Blanca participated only very passively while she tried to plan a goodbye that wouldn't hurt anyone's feelings, Tere took a large whalebone corset from the mountain of complicated attire she'd discarded, and said to Blanca:

"Help me put it on."

"On whom?"

"On Almanza."

The idea of seeing the count of Almanza naked except for Tere's corset made her burst out laughing; she choked on the champagne and it came out her nose as she coughed. Almanza and Tere clapped her on the back until she could breathe again. The gentleman's vigor was renewed with Tere's proposition.

"How exciting to see you in a corset!" Blanca said, clapping.

The two naked women held the apparatus open, and Almanza got inside. They raised it to his waist so that the only protruding parts were his hairy pectorals, his behind, and his equally hairy private parts, which swelled as the two women pulled on the ribbons to tighten the corset.

"He has the wasp waist of a marquise!" laughed Tere.

"A marquise with a mustache," added Blanca, tugging on the ribbons so that what the count lost in thickness at the middle of his anatomy, he gained above and—especially—below. He took his two friends by the waist, and as he paraded around he recited:

> *At a terrace where the branches bent down,*
> *you could catch the tremolo of Aeolian*
> *lyres as they caressed the stemmed gowns*
> *of the many upturned, white magnolias.*
>
> *The marquise Eulalia, haughty and cool,*
> *honored at the same time two rivals,*
> *one was the blond viscount of duels;*
> *the other, the young abbé of madrigals.*

The lithe and mustachioed marquise Eulalia, while the band on the gramophone *loosed its pearls of magic notes*, laughed and laughed and laughed, kissing, first, *the blond viscount of duels*—who was Tere, occupied in caressing his *upturned magnolia*—and then the *young abbé of madrigals,* who was Blanca, also laughing, even though she was bored by the *sobs of cellos,* and though the *soul of a glass of champagne lay buried in her pupils' damp and starry night.* Enough. She had lost interest in the game, like when she was little: I don't want to play anymore! Who did Almanza think he was? She was leaving. Eulalia and the blond viscount, with the *staccato of a dancer* and the *mad fugues of some nameless schoolgirl,* pursued her. Blanca was adamant, and told them:

"I have something urgent I need to do."

Almanza looked so crestfallen with this news that even his handlebar mustache drooped. Tere, on the other hand, who had been trying to bite Blanca's nipples to get her to stay, rose up furiously and cried:

"Sure, you have to visit that two-bit scoundrel, that Archie . . ."

"At least he's a young scoundrel, who doesn't need a corset to do what he does."

There it is, thought Blanca. Everything has been said now. Enough. Almanza coughed, caressing the bare back of the little marquise paused in the doorway between the bedroom and the salon. He defended himself:

"Frankly, my dear Blanca, I don't believe you can complain of my performance . . ."

"Certainly not. I merely complain that it *is* a performance. So no, don't cry, Tere . . . Don't cry, Almanza, you're both charming and I adore you, but . . ."

They begged her not to leave, pleaded with her to stay, promised to supply her with all the pleasures and excitements possible, said the three of them could run away to Tangiers, to the Bosphorus, to the lights of New York or simply to Paris, but that it was wrenching to see how the years passed and first the marquess and then Paquito and now Blanca sat there atop a fortune that no one used and that could end up in the hands of a rogue like this Archie. They begged while a haughty Blanca donned her lovely chiffon. She closed the front door feeling sorry for them, but, above all, deathly bored.

On the other hand, upon opening the door to her darkened bedroom, her heart gave such a startled leap in her chest that it almost took her breath away: there were the two eyes like two moons swimming in that infinite space, dark and hot and aromatic. She perceived a new horizon of potent smells, primitive and elemental. She did not turn on the light. The eyes came slowly closer in the darkness until she saw the very depths of those hollow pupils, the other side of those orbs whose iridescence made drops of saliva shine on the snout, which was growling. His growl suddenly rising, Luna lunged at her, pushing her to the floor onto shards of broken crystal bottles, hitting her with his rough paws, stripping her again with his boiling-hot muzzle, biting her as if about to devour her satiny flesh, her perfect breasts, her trembling thighs, his fangs sinking into her arms as snarls boiled out of his snout. Why hadn't Archibaldo explained the dog's absence from his house? Why hadn't she explained the dog's presence in hers? Why must Luna be incapable of explaining himself, of decoding himself to unite the two of them? There were those two eyes, limpid like two blank continents, like unwritten pages, like paths never traveled, two gray-gold depths that expressed nothing because they merely *were*, into which Blanca's mind could sink down and dissolve, or else find something that she couldn't quite see from this side of the twin moons. When the dog realized that Blanca was dissolving in that night's first spasm, he let her go. Blanca, naked before the unknown, fled to take refuge in the bathroom, where she locked herself in and turned on the light. The dog scratched at the wood and growled. But he was on the other side of the door, a denizen of that destruction and chaos and of the unknown, where he reigned as king. In her bathroom, an exhausted Blanca placed her softest towels in the bathtub, and, after turning out the light, got into that clean bed and fell asleep.

The next day, as she heard Luna running madly about in the room next door, the earthquake of the curtains falling, his ferocious howling, his paws, his insistent claws scratching and scratching at the door with a strength that could knock it down, Blanca began to dress herself. But when she entered her dressing room naked and sore and looked at herself in the mirrors, she realized she could not go to Archibaldo's, as she'd planned, so that he could help her free herself from a curse that merely returning the dog would not dispel. She saw her alabaster body stained with bruises and welts, striped with scratches, clearly marked by the beast's fangs, making her into a sort of tenebristic, *tremendista*, and tragic saint, a horrific and bloody martyr who must, above all, be hidden away: she couldn't go ask Archibaldo for help— though he was the only one who could help her—because he would want to undress her, and then ... She had to wait. How long? And with that monster destroying the universe in the neighboring room, that elemental force unleashed in the form of the single reiterated, unknown question in that empty pair of eyes? How long should she wait to go and clear things up with that ... That scoundrel? No. That ... something, but not scoundrel: she could think of accusations, but they would be more serious than that. The dog had fallen silent. This time, without a window to the outside in her bathroom and the Patek Philippe in a sorry state, she had no idea what time of the day or night it might be. In the bedroom, the dog had not whined in a good while. Why not? Wasn't it preferable for him to growl than to remain in this silence, which was as terrible as the nothing of his eyes, the color of twilit water? Blanca pressed her ear to the door. When she didn't hear Luna on the other side, and after ruling out the idea that he could have fled or jumped into the garden, she opened the door: he was standing on his hind legs and peering out the window. He seemed utterly concentrated on something he saw outside. After a little while, Hortensia knocked at her door.

"Madame Marquise ... Madame Marquise ... there's a somewhat strange man downstairs ... he says his name is Archibaldo Arenas. He insists it's urgent that he speak with you, ma'am."

So he had come to her? For what? To ask for her hand in marriage so they could have a bunch of children? To account for his affairs with a list that would start with the unorthodox Tere Castillo? To take the dog? Wasn't he capable of giving her even that? Was the wretch so incapable of giving anything ... ? And now he wanted to snatch away the fever of the two pale, inalterable eyes that he used first to hypnotize and then to betray after switching them for a pair of simple, though beautiful and lively, black eyes? Was he anything more than an illusionist who promised happiness only to never deliver? And now he intended to take away Luna, whom he hadn't even asked about the other day? What could he understand about that terrible and wonderful dog into whose pupils she could sink in a way she could never sink into the painter's black pupils, or anyone else's? Oh, not that. If he wanted to see her, let him be patient while she got dressed. Let him wait downstairs. She would give him a piece of her mind. She locked herself in the bathroom again while the dog, in enthralled silence, hung his head out the window. She planned, above all, to deny the gray dog's existence to anyone who claimed he was there, accusing them of hallucinating if they complained of any barking or of gargoyles in her window.

In the bathroom she chopped off her hair with a pair of scissors and a razor, cruelly, roughly, until her head resembled an impish child's. In spite of the clear mistakes in the cut, she couldn't deny that Tere Castillo would have called her appearance "just ducky, really..." Her whole body, aching and bruised, was one big wound. She chose her most unrevealing dress, dark and sad. She opened her swan-embossed compact to dust herself in a cloud of rice powder that turned her pale. For a moment she considered carrying, in her purse, her gold Baby Browning with its mother of pearl grip, an indispensable accessory for so many ladies these days. Or else a little vial of acid to deform his pretty, treacherous face that promised everything and gave nothing, and on top of it all came to take away what little she possessed. But no: the truth was she did not love him. She would only carry one of those weapons in her bag if she loved him. But she did not, because her interior was an empty continent.

She went down the marble staircase amid poor Hortensia's unintelligible exclamations, closely watched by the cranes in the stained glass window. But her buttoned-up dress and thick black stockings hid her wounds, those of her body and her soul, neither of which she was willing to display. Though she was pale, the only thing she felt like showing the world — which would understand all this even less than she did herself — was the figure of a widow, young and sad but

93

whole: a little widow who, in short, had nothing of Lehár about her, the sort of widow of which the Mamertos of the world would approve, and of which the Sosa line no doubt had countless examples, off in Alarcón de los Arcos.

Archibaldo was waiting for her downstairs, his slouch hat in hand and one foot on the bottom step. She felt such boredom upon seeing his imploring black eyes which lacked the essential thing—which perhaps was no more than the reflection of a certain twilight, in a certain place at a certain moment in both of their lives—but she could not quite convince herself that this boredom was as definitive and harrowing as the boredom she'd felt the night before in the house of her good friend the count of Almanza. She stopped a few steps before reaching the landing, so that Archibaldo had to look up to address her.

"Blanca . . ." he murmured.

"Did you wish to speak with me, sir?"

"Please, Blanca . . ."

"Is this about an advance for the portrait of my deceased husband, the marquess of Loria, may he rest in peace?"

This man wasn't even a salaried servant who could be of some use to her, like the troop of Mamertos. Let him be gone. She had no dog at all. No dog existed. It was necessary to erase Luna's existence, to leave no room for questions to be asked about him, to refuse before the request came, to leave no opening, because she could no longer live without Luna's pale, empty eyes. The only thing she wanted was for this painter to leave her house as soon as possible. Why hadn't she gone to the Ritz last night, as she'd planned, and saved herself this whole scene? No. Luna could not be left alone. He needed her, just as she needed him, because the two of them were like light, each reflected in the mirror of the other. What was clear was that she did not need this man or his possessive expression, this man who couldn't even hear Luna's crazed barking, locked in her filthy, ruined room. She was not willing to hand him over, no matter what demands were made.

Archibaldo gazed at her incredulously, speechless before this absolutely unexpected incarnation of Blanca. Yes. His eyes, as on that first day, were simple, hard tar: decipherable, avid. Was he angry? Well, then, let him get angry. Defiant, Blanca took another step down, not speaking, holding his gaze as if some part of her had not lost the hope that another twilight would turn them—even if only fleetingly—a lemon-gray color once more. He did not speak either, but not because he refused, like Blanca, but rather because, for some absurd reason that she wasn't going to trouble herself to understand, he could not: in sum, he was a slave to his own smallness. Blanca, to demonstrate that he had not left her mute, said:

"Why must you come bother me over this matter, instead of taking these trivialities straight to Don Mamerto Sosa, whose notary offices take care of and administer all of my wealth and make all my payments?"

Archibaldo waited a second, his eyes boring into her. Then he put on his hat and murmured:

"Certainly, I'll do just that."

And he hurried out of the palazzo, as though trying to hold in an explosion until he was outside and so as not to cause any destruction to Blanca's house.

Mechanically, she turned around as soon as she heard the door slam. With her delicate fingers brushing the railing, she began to ascend again. Ultimately, the little painter was quite a charming boy, as well as polite—aside from that slam of the door, which she didn't like one bit. It hadn't even occurred to him to ask for the dog that belonged to him, though he must have heard the barking that was, indeed, booming in her ears. But as she ascended, before reaching the top of the stairs, she considered the pretensions of the man she had just sent away:

"What a laugh!" she said to herself as she opened the door to her bedroom, once so beautiful, now this fetid and satisfying ruin.

8

THE LEGEND IS STILL SPREAD THROUGH MADRID — THUS
far never disproven, only uttered in whispers and only every so often,
and which no one will admit to believing until the next incident—that
couples who drive into Retiro Park at dusk to make love are often
harrowed by a panic-inducing sight: at the moment just before climax,
suddenly, in the car window, the big gray head of a giant dog with
shining gray-gold eyes appears, a drooling tongue hanging from the
panting muzzle that barks and barks, front paws up on the window,
until the two terrified lovers manage to untangle themselves and start
the car and flee at top speed from that terror that hadn't figured into
their tender calculations: the girl in a river of tears or a fit of hysterics,
the man flooring the accelerator and heeding only the barking of the
dog chasing them, which, as the car speeds away, fades into the noise
of the urban distance. Few are the couples whose love survives this
test. No one has ever been able to find that dog, not even the police,
who haven't looked very hard, because with things the way they are
now, of course, they have to concern themselves with more serious
problems. Nor have the park guards been successful, though they
have occasionally set out to investigate how much truth there could be
behind the sinister murmurings that, year after year, are persistently
renewed, but which, at the end of the day, have every appearance
of being inspired by a hysterical hallucination—but which, it must
be admitted, may be more than just the product of shared fantasies.

After the painter left her house that day, Blanca was only able to stay in her room because Luna was focused on barking out the window with his paws up on the sill. She sat down on the edge of her ruined bed, on the gutted mattress, looking at the beast's gray, upright back, skinnier now because she hadn't fed him in days: Luna was hungry. That was why he barked. But he didn't run from her side: he had seized her bedroom for himself. Hunger was too simple a reason to explain behavior as singular as this dog's. And so, during the course of the afternoon, Blanca was able to stay there staring at nothing, her attention focused solely on the pain of the inflamed bite marks burning her muscles, her back, her arms. A while later, Hortensia knocked at her door. When she heard the marquise reply, she said, very quietly and even more respectfully than usual:

"Madame Marquise?"

"Yes, Hortensia?"

"The marquise Doña Casilda is here."

"Have her wait in the Chinese salon. Prepare a table for us to take tea there, and serve it. I will be down in just a moment. Tell her to please wait for me."

"Yes, Madame Marquise."

Why not go down immediately? After all, she was dressed appropriately, and that was the most important thing, of course, because it was what others would see. She couldn't deny that it was boring to spend so many hours sitting on the edge of her bed staring into space, waiting for Luna to turn back toward her and allow her to once again behold the emptiness of his yellow eyes. She felt, however, the great satisfaction of having had the strength to send away Archibaldo and the mirage he embodied, and to remain, as was fitting, alone with Luna and whatever he might give her. The wounds and scratches from his paws and teeth hurt a lot now, as if her glowing flesh, which in another time had had murderous pretensions, were starting now to decompose and die. But she would not go down to Casilda yet because it was important to impose a theatrical rhythm on the thing, regulating entrances and exits as if skillfully directing a scene, as if nothing were true, everything pure calculation, pure artifice, pure representation: in this way, it all hurt less, and the beasts were only part of the stage set, like the swan in *Lohengrin*. What's more, she wouldn't have come off well if, as soon as she heard that her mother-in-law was there, she had run downstairs shouting with glee like a real bumpkin of a daughter-in-law, hugging and kissing Casilda to welcome her back from Paris. After a carefully measured time, Blanca emerged from her bedroom, turning the key in the lock with Luna inside. She went down to the little salon and the waiting marquise Doña Casilda, who upon seeing her stood up with open arms and cried:

"What a joy to be back! I'm exhausted! Not from the trip, but from the dreary bore of a sermon at mass this morning."

And she hugged and kissed her daughter-in-law, who said: "Casilda! How lovely! And what a fabulous dress. Lanvin?"

"No. Callot."

"Of course, Callot, I see it now . . ."

They spent a good while exchanging pleasantries about the news from Paris, what people were wearing and what they'd stopped wearing, how everyone except Spanish women were now summering in Deauville and not Biarritz. Casilda had seen Sacha Guitry dining with Yvonne Printemps at the next table over at La Tour d'Argent, and she was much prettier than onstage, and much more of a lady, and this summer white was back with a vengeance: everything was white, furniture, rugs, houses, cars, dresses both cocktail and evening, and, obviously, sports clothes.

"To be sure," Casilda added as she took a sip of tea without looking at her interlocutor, as if she were saying something utterly insignificant, "I've heard you were just seen in white, wearing a short tennis skirt the other day, I think over near Plaza Chamberí. The queens of France wear white in mourning, my dear, not mere Spanish marquises like us . . ."

"They say it's also the color of mourning for Chinese ladies. I feel foreign as a Chinese woman here in Madrid, Casilda, without Paquito."

This time her mother in law scrutinized her openly. "Are you sure you don't have consolations or pastimes that are more or less entertaining . . . ?"

Under a hat adorned with the most elegant aigrette, Casilda's head was magnificence itself: she was unshakable beauty, carved in alabaster, the kind of beauty of closed eyes in tombs that lasts through the ages, but lacks the passion of the fleeting beauty that emerges from freshness and joy and elasticity and sparkle, moving beauty that exists only during a very brief moment of glory, as if the being to which it belonged had entered a spotlight, paused for a second, and then left it behind for-evermore. That was the case of Blanca's beauty; it was what made her so tender, so succulent. Casilda found herself wondering how much longer it would last, because today she thought Blanca seemed out of sorts and pallid. It wouldn't take many years for her to become just like her fat mother. Blanca held her eyes as she answered the question.

"I think perhaps Mario could give me driving lessons. As a distrac-tion. Then I would buy a coupe like Tere's so I could feel completely independent."

"I turn my back for a second and Tere starts to dominate your life! You're so unfaithful to me!"

"Unfaithful, always. Disloyal, never."

A very slight blush lit the mother marquise's face for a second. She took a piece of toast and continued:

"In any case, it doesn't matter. Tere has been my best friend for years, and she tells me everything."

"And does Almanza also tell you everything?"

"Indeed he does."

"Interesting. Have you seen them already?"

"Certainly. Don't get the idea that I would come see you before visiting my lover."

Blanca flushed at Casilda's brutally direct reply. She also felt fear, because it meant that not only did Casilda know something—which Blanca couldn't care less about—but also that she had something she wanted to talk about. She put a wedge of lemon in her tea and took a sip. "How lovely, the way Almanza sings the fandangos from his homeland!"

"Quit the nonsense. It's been years since Almanza was my lover.

I'm talking about Tere."

This time, instead of turning red—aware as she was that this would mean repeating a display of naiveté—Blanca dropped the sugar tongs to the floor. Both women leaned over at the same time to pick them up. Below, hidden by the long tablecloth, Casilda, the statuesque, official beauty, the kind that appears engraved on ancient coins or stamped on high-denomination bills, grabbed Blanca's wrist fiercely, her nails digging in. Without sitting up, caressing her daughter-in-law's forehead with her rigid aigrette, she whispered hysterically:

"Let's go. Let's run away, the three of us. To Paris. Tere is crazy about you. So am I."

Blanca sat up. Her delicate hands—which Luna had spared, as he spared everything visible—restored symmetry to the little tray of hors d'oeuvre and the pastry tray in relation to the steep-necked vase containing only a single rose. She said to Casilda, "You haven't mentioned my haircut."

"Just awful!"

"What?"

"*À la garçonne* is one thing, hacked off with scissors is another. It looks like you had a fight with the washerwoman next door and she won."

"It's hard for me to win a fight."

Blanca felt a live, silky thing searching out her foot beneath the tablecloth: Casilda's own bare foot caressing her ankle with stunning skill, running up her aching calves, making incursions under her skirt, seeking to seductively probe between thighs that she—for the moment and as long as it was convenient—kept obstinately closed as she nibbled at a pastry.

"Would you like me to ring for some more hot tea?"

Casilda abandoned all semblance of composure. Gesticulating as she talked and drank cup after cup of lukewarm tea, her aigrette rivaled the eloquence of her beautiful hands. How the three of them should leave together—come, don't be silly, now—and go off to live in Paris! No, Almanza didn't matter at all. What he really liked were chambermaids from his own Atlantic Andalusia, not ladies: their whole relationship had been a farce for years. And this Archie character, come on, a middling little painter, she shouldn't fool herself, he was a naive, mawkish romantic. If Blanca liked artists so much she could get her fill of them in Paris, because it seemed like that plague had come to stay and these days you saw nothing else in the city, sometimes even in the good restaurants. What's that, how did she know . . . well, how had she found out about Blanca and Archibaldo? Oh, Blanca, don't be daft: all of Madrid — and may this finally convince her that this so-called capital was nothing more than a two-horse town just like Alarcón de los Arcos — already knew of her affair with Archibaldo Arenas, that wretched copycat of Anglada Camarasa, himself a copycat, and poor Archie copied whoever he could just to come up with an idea, because oh, the poor thing didn't have a single one of his own. And he believed himself another Domergue . . . ! He'd need a little more *culot* for that! All of Madrid, moreover, had seen her go into his house in Plaza de Chamberí — Casilda could cite the day and hour — dressed for tennis: people said she was a real dish, but there was no denying it was madness to go out dressed like that on the way to her lover's house and expect no one to notice. She, Casilda, would just love to see Blanca in that outfit . . . and her big toe, with such autonomy and agility that it was like she had two extra phalanges, was so effective that it managed to burrow between Blanca's sensitive thighs and reach her tender pelt, which she let Casilda pet while the aigrette went on accentuating her mother-in-law's frivolous commentary. Blanca kept her teacup to her lips so as to hide the expression — painful rictus or smile of pleasure? — of her mouth. Blanca, in spite of the pain that foot was causing as it pressed on the wounds Luna had inflicted, managed to say: "You're afraid I'll marry him."

"Because our fortune would evaporate?"

"Yes: that is, *my* fortune, still. You're worried Archibaldo and I would carry it all off to Nicaragua, where no one would know my painter husband was an imitator of Anglada Camarasa . . . and where he'll be considered a great genius of contemporary painting."

Casilda's foot fell from the sweet footrest it had finally found: she let out a peal of laughter that made Blanca tremble. "But . . . do you take me for an idiot?"

Blanca stammered, "From your laughter I see I have no reason to."

Casilda, sarcastic, hurtful, explained to her that the Mamertos of today weren't the same as the Mamerto of yore. Superficially—and, unfortunately, in certain intimate aspects that they must have inherited from their father—they all *looked* alike. But the morals of today, to say nothing of morale, had changed a lot, becoming, let's say, more flexible, making room for more points of view, a variety of attitudes. Blanca's recent threat to liquidate everything and take off for Nicaragua—neither Almanza nor Tere knew about that part: Casilda was only telling her so she could see just how out-and-out silly she was—had accelerated what more than one person would consider the moral breakdown of the Sosa family: terrified at the threat that this American girl would fritter away the Loria wealth, which ultimately was the only thing they truly respected, they had notified her of the venture to export the fortune to Nicaragua. Casilda—who, by the way, had had the foresight to reach an understanding years ago with the Mamerto currently heading the family—convinced him, if Blanca proved difficult, to make certain papers disappear and others appear that would appoint her, the mother marquise—based on the fact that the younger marquise had not provided heirs, which automatically made Casilda the head of the Loria household—as the inheritor of the family fortune. Blanca, flabbergasted, only managed to offer the plate of pastries to her mother-in-law, who took one and declared: "God, in his infinite mercy, makes an allowance that what one eats on Sunday does not make one fat."

"They're made by the nuns. Good, right . . . ?"

"Delicious."

"So, your invoices from Paris were finally paid?"

"All of them."

"And Almanza's horse?"

"That too. And Tere's theater box."

"Nice watch. Patek Philippe?"

"No. Vacheron."

"I prefer Patek Philippe."

"Vacheron for me."

"How about that."

Casilda's foot, as if seeking an agreement, an alliance, delved again into Blanca's thicket, and the mother marquise's eyes — as she lit a cigarette in her very long holder — were heavy with kohl and passion.

Blanca clamped her thighs shut, because none of this mattered to her at all. She wanted to go see Luna. She stood up. The marquise Doña Casilda looked at her Vacheron, saying, Oh! but how late it had gotten! She always stayed longer than planned when visiting her dear daughter-in-law! They said goodbye with a kiss on the cheek at the palazzo's front door. Casilda, when she kissed her, also caressed Blanca's back a little — as though to console her, perhaps — right in the spot where Luna had left her most bruised. While the servant held the door open, before she went down the steps, Casilda, smiling, turned around to say to Blanca: "All of these arrangements . . . well, they mean that you cannot buy half of Nicaragua, which, I've been told, was your intention. It's too big: more than a fiefdom from ages past. But perhaps you could buy a modest piece of land in El Salvador, which I'm told is smaller. Everything has been arranged for you to have enough to cover that. I'm telling you this so you start getting the idea: the difference, though you may not think it much, is, my dear, enormous. Don't I know it! Oh! It's raining and I didn't bring my umbrella. One just never knows in springtime . . . Really, one never knows anything. *Au revoir, beauté!*"

When Blanca had locked herself once again in her room, she leaned her elbows beside Luna's front paws on the sill of the open window, where she could watch the drizzling rain and while away the time listening to the dog fill the city night with his bestial howling: his eyes, which contained light but did not project it, seemed like the just the right touch to make the gradually falling night into a real, true night.

Was he barking so much out of hunger? Luna was young, voracious, always ravenous: it was one of the things that scared her, and yet also drew her to him. Or was he barking only because he'd spent too long locked up in this room? There was no way to please or satiate him.

"Do you want to go out, Luna?"

The dog, accepting the invitation implicit in the question, started to prance joyfully around Blanca like on that first day: once again a puppy and not a beast. In the darkness of the room those eyes, which promised all because they had nothing, followed her movements as she prepared to go out. Since it was hot out in spite of the rain, Blanca donned only her black oilcloth cloche with a silver buckle over the ear. She also picked up a small purse, in which she carried her Baby Browning with its mother-of-pearl handle. Descending the marble steps with her gray dog at her side, she felt that her authority over the servants was such that it really did erase the dog by her side, and they, obedient, did not see him descending step by step with his mistress. Hortensia waved goodbye nonchalantly from the balustrade upstairs, but Blanca did not wave back. The same with the porter: to them, because she wished it so, Luna did not exist.

"To Retiro," she told Mario before closing the glass that separated them — but only after listening with the patience of a great lady to the driver's admonitions and suggestions. At this hour, and in this rain? Wasn't it dangerous . . . or sad? Wouldn't the lady prefer he take her for an outing somewhere else, along Gran Vía, perhaps, which must be very festive today, a Friday? Of course, with this drizzle that was turning into rain it might all be deserted. These were the things that Mario dared say to her, because they displayed an acceptable interest, a concern for Blanca's person. But he didn't dare show any indignation that the dog sitting next to her in the back seat could sully the car he had tended with such passionate meticulousness ever since he'd been sent from Italy when they bought it. Passing by Don Mamerto's office on the corner of Goya, Blanca felt tempted — fondling the Baby Browning in her purse — to order Mario to stop so she could get out, go up to the Sosas' office, and, after raping the Mamerto on duty, the one with whom Casilda had "an understanding," shoot all the Mamertos in the world with its bullets. But it was such an effort to lower the glass . . . And what would she do with Luna? Bring him up with her, or leave him waiting down here, with Mario? No. Too complicated. Best to continue on to Retiro.

No one was out in the rainy park at that hour of the malignant night. Mario drove slowly, aware that this was a jaunt with no fixed destination or clear purpose, leaning cautiously over the steering wheel to peer closely at everything as if he were afraid of hurting someone — or as if he hoped to? In the long cones of light that extended from the headlamps, the falling rain was like the beaded silver fringe on one of her evening dresses. Pretty. So pretty, right Luna? When they reached the most remote corner, she rolled down the glass between them to ask Mario to stop and open her door. He did so, holding onto the handle and doffing his cap, though he respectfully blocked her way out.

"Will the Madame Marquise get out in this rain?" he inquired.

The driver was tall, strapping, a Romanesco youth with a broken nose and square jaw, with powerful arms and legs squeezed into his spats: with him watching out for her, she had nothing to fear.

"Shall we go for a walk, Luna? Come on . . ."

The driver cleared his throat before speaking, without moving away from the door or letting go of its handle.

"If the Madame Marquise will allow me, I'd advise you not to stray very far from the car's headlamps."

Before getting out, Blanca and the dog questioned the driver, the dog only with his eyes, she with her words. "Why not?"

"There could be bad people."

"What a ridiculous idea, right in the center of Madrid!"

"When we were driving in, didn't the marquise see shapes lurking behind the trees and the monuments?"

Blanca looked him up and down. She told him firmly: "Let us out."

The driver, then, bowing his head a little and opening the door further, made way. Why was this impertinent man opposed to her doing as she pleased? What right did he have to question her, to place the breadth of his shoulders between her and the total darkness where only the stilled moons of Luna's eyes could exist? She yearned to see the dormant lake at this hour. What color was its water at night? Would the Crystal Palace be like a giant square bubble under the pallor of the city sky amid so much darkness, so much silence? What did the swans do at night? Where did they take shelter? And the colorful little boats, in which women like Hortensia were rowed about on Sundays by their boyfriends, men like Mario? And Don Alfonso atop his column, so friendly and rain-soaked, poor fellow? Why did Mario stand there like a guardian or a jailer between her and her desires? Opening her purse, she showed him the Baby Browning.

"Plus, I have this to defend myself with."

"That's not enough, Madame Marquise. There are gypsies. I swear, I saw a bonfire under the trees and a group of ragged silhouettes around it."

"I didn't see a thing."

Blanca dodged Mario's defensive shape to have her way. He reached out to grab her brutally by the wrist. She turned around to slap him under Luna's approving gaze, but then she didn't do it. Instead, she kissed him on the mouth, her desirous lips feeling their desire and dampness reflected on his inferior lips as she pressed her body, wet and confused from the rain, to his, and he responded by delving his tongue into her avid mouth, drinking the raindrops collected in the spiral shells of her ears and on her neck, his mouth following the drops that ran down along her collarbone, yes, yes, she felt him shiver pressed against her, trembling with something that was not fear nor cold but rather a blaze that made them back up in an embrace to the car that awaited them with open doors. Mario pushed Blanca onto the back seat, where the masters rode. Blanca had forgotten—and this time it was true forgetfulness, not an intentional act—to put on underwear, so that when her skirt came up and she opened her vibrant, bruised thighs the driver lunged at her, panting like an animal, sharp-eyed and accurate, and he filled up every particle of her being—her twin breasts like polished moons; her behind, whose pleasures reverberated in her sensitive neck beneath the cloche; her mouth, suffocated by his frenzy—while Luna, who had jumped into the driver's seat and had his paws up on the backrest, put his big, ferocious head through the lowered glass and barked and barked. Blanca gazed into his two pale eyes while the driver raped her with her consent; she sank into those lagoons of crepuscular water as she moaned with pleasure, threatening the driver with police and jail time but clinging to him and squeezing his sex with her own so he wouldn't withdraw, scratching him with her nails, but he went on kissing her and thrusting into her until he made her cry out and join in with the dog's barking in this solitary corner of the park, in the night that was verdant and wild like a tropical night right here in the middle of the city, while this stranger whose violence she detested was making her feel what she could only allow Luna's pale eyes to see her feel, until the driver's brutal vigor, with no need to warn her first, with no need for any words at all, reached the height of pleasure with the same violence and at the same time as her.

He moved off of her as soon as she had fulfilled her function, as if he didn't want Blanca to go on enjoying him when he no longer had any need for her: he pulled away from the embrace and his body went cold. Luna, realizing it was all over, jumped out of the front seat and started to bark and prance outside the open door from which the lovers' legs had protruded just a few seconds before. He was calling her, urging her to follow him, inviting her. Mario, who didn't seem to see or hear the dog, stood up first. He sat in the seat that corresponded to him, a chauffeur, then put his cap back on and lit a cigarette. He stared straight ahead, exhaling smoke without paying any attention to the little marquise as she lowered her skirt, smoothed her hair, and adjusted the oilcloth cloche with its silver buckle, pulling it down on her head: good for the rain, she reflected. And, collecting her purse, she stood up outside to disobey Mario and follow the dog, who seemed to offer something more.

Mario, whose intention was to completely ignore her, couldn't help but feel a quiver of admiration as he watched her pass through the beams of the Isotta Fraschini's headlights striped by the fringe of rain: she was beautiful, slender, thrillingly desirable and untouchable, crossing through the light holding onto her hat with one gloved hand so the newly risen wind wouldn't blow it off, and, hanging from the crook of her elbow, the minuscule purse that scarcely had room for a compact along with the Baby Browning.

Before she disappeared into the bushes, however, it seemed to Mario that he saw a ferocious shadow emerge from the darkness, an animal, a monster, something terrifying that leapt to assault her with what was—he later declared, to the incredulous laughter of all—a clear intention to devour her. The driver left the car immediately, running toward Blanca to free her from that strange beast, even though he was unprepared to defend someone else or himself against such an unimaginable danger. Then he heard a gunshot.

"Brava!" the driver exclaimed in admiration of the Madame Marquise's cool head.

He went on searc'hing, terrified and desperate, recruiting the few people he found in the park at that hour to join his search, all of them shouting, but no one found either the marquise or the supposed animal. The only thing his eyes landed upon, a few steps beyond the edge of the headlights' beams, was the tiny golden Baby Browning with the mother-of-pearl handle. He picked it up, got into the Isotta Fraschini, and sped to the nearest police station, where he relayed what this story's author has just narrated in this chapter that is reaching its end; only, he did not mention the gray dog. The police commandeered the luxurious car, word was sent to the family and the proper authorities and the park guards so they could immediately begin an exhaustive search that lasted all that rainy night and all the next day under a sunny, porcelain sky, but the beautiful marquise of Loria never appeared, and neither did the gigantic animal whose ferocious shadow the driver tried in vain to describe convincingly to the jury, and on whom he was trying to place blame for the murder. The only things found in the search were the silver buckle from the cloche, one French shoe, and the gold Patek Philippe, which proved that this had been no robbery but rather a crime of passion, incriminating Mario and keeping him in prison for a term that lasted many years due to the ruthlessness with which the mother marquise, Doña Casilda, pursued the case against him: her beloved daughter-in-law, she said, was all she had left in the world. This Mario person could keep that story of ferocious animals that no one had ever seen to himself.

For a time people believed that the little marquise of Loria would reappear, but she never did. The fortune of the House of Loria passed as a matter of course to Casilda, since Blanca had left no children, and whatever dark arrangements Paquito had come to with Don Mamerto the elder, the marquise fixed with a younger Don Mamerto who had a more modern mentality. He behaved so well in the whole dirty affair, to which even the newspapers added their two cents, that Casilda put her considerable society influences to use, reaching His Majesty himself to suggest he consider the possibility of distinguishing the ancient and honorable Sosa line with a title.

Everyone celebrated how Casilda honored her daughter-in-law's memory by providing for the girl's family. When ex-minister Arias arrived in Madrid to investigate his daughter's devastating disappearance and prevent the rapist or kidnapper from going free, he was summoned by Don Mamerto Sosa to receive what was rightly his. He traveled in the company of his daughter Charo, who fit quite nicely into her sister's clothing, which she planned to flaunt in Managua as soon as the mourning period was over. The painter Archibaldo Arenas was caught up in the red tape of the investigation and trial because he'd been about to begin portraits of Blanca and Paquito — the latter commissioned by Don Mamerto Sosa — and had visited the victim at the palazzo the very afternoon of her disappearance. Between one thing and the other the painter fell in love with Charo, who was quite beautiful — though perhaps not the equal of her sister, since she was much darker-skinned — and the father, who had another three beauties he would need to marry off, stayed in Madrid longer than he'd planned in order to take care of the inheritance and other matters.

As for our friend the count of Almanza, Casilda considered him to be past his prime and she put him out to pasture, spending a pittance to buy up some lands for him around Huelva. He turned out to be not quite the layabout everyone thought him and he developed the land, building a club with a mini-golf course and a bar, with which, even if it didn't make him immediately rich, he felt satisfied enough—now that he was in the area of Spain that produced the maids who drove him mad with their fandangos—that he often wrote to his old friend Casilda to tell her of his ventures, and even took her on as an investor when his business expanded. Casilda, in the company of Almanza's cousin, Tere Castillo, went off to live in Paris definitively, for Madrid was nothing but a big village, and Paris, on the other hand, was the capital of the world. There, the two friends grew old together, happy, never losing that peculiar Andalusian accent to their French, both of them dressed in tailored gray flannel suits, their hair cut *à la garçonne* even many years after it had gone out of style, wearing flat-heeled shoes, ties, and Basque berets—which, they claimed, they were the first to introduce in the elegant circles they frequented. Their strolls along the Bois in the mornings kept them always thin, and they lived many years with no mishaps.

And to end on another happy note it must be added that ex-minister Arias, after having previously married off his poor departed eldest daughter to a Spanish grandee, now had the pleasure of giving away his second daughter, his beloved Charo, to the painter Archibaldo Arenas, who, even if he could not boast a noble title, did boast the—to Arias, very illustrious—title of artist. With the money he received from Blanca's disappearance—and it must be said that through it all the marquise Doña Casilda behaved with extraordinary generosity, facilitating all the paperwork via the intervention of the distinguished notary Don Mamerto Sosa—he was able to buy, as a dowry for his daughter, the apartment where Archibaldo lived in the Plaza de Chamberí, where the couple set up house. Archibaldo's personal warmth, the rich range of his palette, his versatility, and his close relationships with persons of high social positions, soon made him into one of most sought-after portraitists in noble circles.

The ex-minister headed back to Nicaragua once the wedding was over, pleased that even in those days, when he'd had to tighten his belt, he'd been lucky enough to dower his second daughter. How would he provide for the remaining three? Well, he would cross that bridge when he came to it.

Just as Archibaldo had always wanted, he and Charo had many children. Sometimes the painter thought of poor Blanca, who'd been so much less passionate than his Charo. But as the years passed her image faded, and even though they named their first daughter Blanca in memory of the disappeared sister, with time he didn't even think of her when he and Charo brought their troop of little ones to row in boats or go for a stroll in Retiro Park, with Luna, his big, ever-faithful gray dog at his heels.

MADRID
OCTOBER 1979–JANUARY 1980